W9-APW-159

Ophie out of Oz

Kathleen O'Dell

illustrations by Rosie Winstead

Dial Books
New  York

Published by Dial Books
A member of Penguin Group (USA) Inc.
345 Hudson Street
New York, New York 10014

Designed by Teresa Kietlinski
Text set in Dutch
Printed in the U.S.A. on acid-free paper

1 3 5 7 9 10 8 6 4 2

Library of Congress Cataloging-in-Publication Data
O'Dell, Kathleen, date.
Ophie out of Oz / Kathleen O'Dell;
illustrations by Rosie Winstead.
p.   cm.
Summary: Fourth grader Ophelia Peeler has
always felt that she was just like Dorothy in Oz,
skipping down the yellow brick road, until a move
to Oregon, away from her best friend,
sends her on a different path.
ISBN 0-8037-2930-8
[1. Moving, Household—Fiction.
2. Best friends—Fiction. 3. Friendship—Fiction.
4. Schools—Fiction.] I. Winstead, Rosie, ill.
II. Title.
PZ7.O2325Op 2004
[Fic]—dc22
2003019399

For Celeste O'Dell—
Mother, writer, and friend,
with love . . .

Chapter One

"Where oh where . . ." wondered Ophie Peeler, looking around her big, almost-empty bedroom, "did Mom pack my ruby slippers?"

She opened a cardboard box and pulled out a cross-eyed elephant by his trunk.

"Well, Toto," she said. "Welcome to Oregon!" She had won Toto at some county fair at least three cities ago.

Ophie placed the elephant in the middle of the room. He appeared tiny and lonely surrounded by bare, neon-pink walls.

"Maybe we'll get used to it, Toto," Ophie said. "Remember my green room? Yick."

She bent over the box and pulled out a red armadillo. "And hello to you *too*, little Toto-rooni," she said.

Ophie once had a small stuffed Scotty dog named Toto that she loved very much. But he got lost in a move between Tucson and Modesto. Now all her animals were named Toto, so that no matter who got lost, there would always be another Toto to take his place.

"Come out, shoes!" Ophie called. She kept digging—tossing out an old Barbie, a cracked flutophone, a scraggly feather boa—until the box was empty. "They have to be here somewhere," she said.

Ophie opened another box. Folded on top was a handmade banner. Ophie smiled, and smoothed it open on the carpet.

✿ The Learning Castle's fourth grade Bungalow H says goodbye to Ophie Peeler!

♪ Farewell to our most enthusiastic performer!
—Mrs. DiLacotto

Goodby Peeler. Knowing you has been like watching some weird TV show. —Eric G.

Ophie I hope you grow up to be a writer because then you can write yourself all the parts and star in all the plays. —Eva H.

You talk alot more than any other girl I know. So I hope people in Oregon like talking. —James Peat

You sure didn't stay very long. —Olivia Enfield

I will miss you more than words can say. Who will make up songs for me on my birthday? Who will act out all the movies on the playground? Who will be the best friend I ever had? I think I want to cry. I WILL cry! —Lizzy Fannon
P.S. You are the best Dorothy of OZ.

Ophie's eyes started to sting. She could still see Lizzy in the backseat of her funky old station wagon, her hand pressed against the glass. In all her moves, no one had ever been so sad to see Ophie go. Not fair, she thought, to never again smell the clove and orangey scent of Lizzy's tiny apartment, or spend any more hot afternoons singing on the stoop.

And it didn't matter that Lizzy didn't have a TV or a computer or anything like that. You could still do the funnest stuff at Lizzy's place. Like decorate her walls with Magic Marker. Or bake a cake for the pigeons out of all the odds and ends in the refrigerator.

Even Lizzy's mom, who looked like Lizzy's grown-up twin, was fun. She seemed to love Ophie too, and would often walk with her arms draped around the girls' shoulders. "I've never seen two more sympathetic personalities," she used to say, giving them both a squeeze.

Ophie picked up a pen and wrote on the poster: *I miss you too, Lizzy Fannon!* She underlined the word *miss* three times.

During the plane trip up here, Ophie saw the palm trees turn into evergreens and the sky get duller and rainier. And all the way, her new baby sister, Callie, croaked and cried while her mother sat looking crabby and exhausted.

Ophie didn't feel at all excited as they approached the new house. Usually she was bursting to see her new bedroom and somersault through the bare rooms. Not this time. This time something was definitely different. No best-ever friend. *No Lizzy*.

"Sweetie!" Ophie's mother broke into her rememberings. "You better get walking. It's a quarter till eight."

"Yeah. Okay."

"School's only five blocks away," her mother said. "That's the nice thing about living here. We won't have to drive so much."

"I wonder if I'll like this one," said Ophie, half to herself.

Mrs. Peeler ran her hand through Ophie's hair. "Oh, I think you'll like it fine. You always do."

"I do always do, don't I?" said Ophie, squaring her shoulders.

"Yep," said Mrs. Peeler. "Just put your head down and charge in. If only we all could be as resilient as you are . . ." Ophie saw her mom stare at the piles of unpacked boxes. It was a tired sort of look she had seen many times.

"I'll be down in a minute, okay?"

Her mother kissed her forehead. "Yes, dear," she said.

Ophie waited until she no longer heard her mother's footsteps. Then she sat on the floor with her fists balled up against her eyes. She made a picture in her head of Margaret Scott Elementary School. This school had gardens with flowers and a sun that almost never stopped shining. Ophie saw herself wearing her ruby red shoes, placing one glittering foot in front of the other, walking slowly at first, then skipping down the yellow brick road . . .

There! She felt it! A magic, electric rush . . . This trick always worked. Ophie opened her eyes and stood up.

"Well then," she said, "here I go!" She picked up her backpack, turned on her heel, and marched down the stairs. When she reached the front door, she hollered up the stairwell, "I'm off to see the wizard, Mom!"

"Good luck, sweetie!" called Mrs. Peeler, giving Ophie a salute.

Waaaaaaahh! Waaaaaahh-hahhh! The baby began to bleat. Ophie covered her ears and skipped out the front door.

Chapter Two

To Ophie's eye, the gray clouds here sagged in the sky like piles of old grandpa underwear. The wet pavement and the wet air smelled like wood shavings and dirt. Was Lizzy walking to school alone today too? Ophie wondered. At least Lizzie still had the hot blue sky and a school draped in vines with purple flowers. Here everything was so quiet that just the clip-clopping of her own footsteps seemed extra loud.

"Except for these words I am sort of singing . . ." she crooned to the shrubbery, "this is the silentest place I've ever been!"

"WHO'S THERE?"

Ophie startled. The voice came from the other side of the hedge.

"Me?" Ophie answered.

The hedge rustled, and a blond, pigtailed head popped out. The squarish head belonged to a big girl with a serious, blue stare.

"What school you go to?"

"Margaret Scott Elementary," Ophie said.

"No you don't." The girl narrowed her eyes. "I go there."

"It's my first day," Ophie said.

"But it's March," the girl said flatly. Her voice seemed to rumble up from deep down in her rib cage.

Ophie was about to explain that yes, people do start school in March when their fathers are salesmen—when another head popped out. This one belonged to a much littler girl with dark eyes as bright and shiny as a squirrel's.

"What grade?" she squeaked.

Ophie stood on her tiptoes. "Not till you tell me how many more you got back there."

"It's just us," said the big girl. She stuck a leg out from the leaves and struggled her way through the branches. She left a hole behind her just right for the little girl to crawl through.

"Brittany Borg," said the big girl, resting her hands on her hips. "And this is my sister, Tana."

"Third grade here," Tana said.

"I'm fourth grade," Brittany said.

"I'm in fourth grade too," Ophie said. She couldn't get over how big and solid Brittany looked. Maybe she flunked a few times. Ophie looked at her watch. "I gotta hurry up."

Brittany followed. "You got any friends yet?"

"No," Ophie said over her shoulder.

"Me neither."

Ophie walked faster.

"That's the school," Brittany called.

"Uh-huh," said Ophie, trying to sound brave. Since Ophie's mother had taken her by on the weekend, the school hadn't gotten any more cheery-looking. The low brick building looked like a factory that made something boring. Like, maybe tires.

"Wait up," said Brittany. "We aren't going to the classroom this morning."

"Why?" Ophie asked.

"We're going to the cafetorium," Brittany said, catching her breath. "To sing."

Ophie stopped. She felt immediately better and more friendly. "You sing?" she asked.

"Yah. They make us," said Brittany. "For a show."

"What show?"

"For the assembly," said Tana. "We have one every month. But it's the fourth graders' turn today."

"Well, I love singing!" said Ophie. "Actually, singing and acting! I love both of 'em." She gazed at the groups of kids streaming through the school's big glass front door.

"Let me show you something," Ophie said. She gathered her thin brown hair into two pigtails and posed, rolling her eyes to the heavens in a dreamy sort of way. "Who am I?"

"I don't know," said Brittany. "You didn't say your name."

Ophie kept the pose. "No, no. Not my real name. I'm *pretending* to be someone. Who am I?"

"Hmmm," Brittany said.

"Hint number one: I look just like her. Hint number two: I sing 'Somewhere Over the Rainbow' . . ."

"I give up," Brittany said.

"I'm DOROTHY. Dorothy of OZ!"

"Oh, yes!" said Tana. "You look *just* like her!"

"I even sang 'Over the Rainbow' for a show at my old school in California. I could sing it for this school too. Eventually. Everyone always tells me there's something extra-special about the way I sing it." Ophie smiled. "People just love that song!"

"Don't think I know that one," Brittany said.

"I do!" said Tana.

"Everybody should!" said Ophie. "It's famous!"

The three girls made their way down a

crowded hall. Ophie looked up and noticed the high ceiling with crisscrossing steam pipes and little steering wheel things. The linoleum was cold and shiny. A chill made her want to cross her arms and hug herself. She whistled instead.

"I have to go to room five," said Tana, "but over there, that's the cafetorium."

Ophie followed Brittany through some double doors to a big room with a stage in front. *Wow.* The stage looked beautiful with its cardboard covered wagon and the big hand-painted banner overhead. WESTWARD HO! it said in red paint. There were risers for the singers to stand on. A swarm of boys and girls carrying tambourines bumped into one another as they took their places.

"Oh, this is just so much . . . better!" Ophie said, bouncing. "Do you ever get that feeling that someone just let you out of a box?"

"Nope," Brittany said.

"Really?" Ophie said. "Well, I do." She paused, shielded her eyes, and surveyed the hundreds of seats. She had never performed in front of an audience this big before.

"So, what song will we be doing first?"

"'Sweet Betsy from Pike,'" Brittany said.

Ophie watched as a lady in a black skirt tried to quiet the crowd. "Is that our teacher?"

"Yah," Brittany said. "She's Miss Fast."

Ophie shot her hand in the air. "Miss Fast! Miss Fast!" she said. "Where should I stand?"

"Oh . . . Ophelia Peeler, am I right?" said her teacher, looking distracted.

"Call me Ophie."

"Ophie, then." Miss Fast smiled. "Well, first of all, welcome. Why don't you just take a seat over here?" Miss Fast pointed to the front row—in the audience.

"But, Miss Fast," Ophie continued. "I can sing in the chorus," she said. "Really! I sang at my old schools all the time . . ."

"But this is your first day," said her teacher. "And I don't have a tambourine for you."

"That's okay. I can just pretend to have a tambourine," said Ophie.

"But you don't know all the songs," said Miss Fast.

"But I can just mouth 'em till I catch on!" said Ophie.

Miss Fast rested her hand on Ophie's shoulder. "Why don't you just sit with me in the front row and watch this time?"

Ophie hung her head for a moment, then said, "Okay. I'm a really good singer, though."

"Oo," said Brittany. "Boy. Too bad."

"I see you've met Brittany Borg," said Miss Fast, leading Ophie to her seat. "She's just been here since September. You know, you two new girls might enjoy getting to know each other."

Ophie nodded politely. She didn't say what she was thinking—she had seen enough of Brittany to already know that was *really* unlikely.

As the rest of the students filed in for the assembly, Ophie looked around. So many kids! Luckily, she'd always found it easy to memorize names and faces.

The piano began to play a waltz—an introduction to the opening number. The fourth-grade chorus banged their tambourines to the beat. *ONE-two-three, ONE-two-three* . . . Ophie watched as a trembling boy in a cowboy hat stepped up to the microphone.

"The pioneers endured many hardships on the Oregon Trail," said the boy, reading from an index card. "They brought with them everything they (*gulp*) owned."

Ophie wondered if the boy was going to faint. She hunkered down in her chair when two girls in pioneer sunbonnets stepped up and took the microphone. Suddenly, the stage was blasted with light.

A man and woman with a big video camera, a fuzzy microphone on a stick, and their own portable spotlight appeared at the front of the stage. They closed in on the girls as they sang: "Oh, do you remember Sweet Betsy from Pike, who crossed the wild mountains with her husband, Ike?"

What a spectacle they made! Ophie could just picture herself and Lizzy up there in those costumes. And were they really wearing stage makeup and rouge? The entire class was backing them up, banging tambourines and singing "Toorah loorah lee-ay!" after every verse.

Ophie listened, with one finger in her ear. They weren't anywhere near as good singers as Ophie and Lizzy. But they were pretty girls. Especially the curly-haired one with the bright, dimpled grin. When the girls' number was over, the lights and camera disappeared. *What gives?* Ophie thought. *Who are they?*

As soon as the audience's final applause died down, Ophie quickly hopped up to the stage. All the students were in a crush, talking. The sunbonnet girls were in the corner. Ophie started to shoulder her way through to them and was suddenly blocked. By Brittany Borg.

"Hey, Peeler," she said. "That your name?"

"That's my LAST name." Ophie tried to push past, but Brittany wouldn't budge. She sighed. "So, Brittany, can you tell me who those girls are? In the hats? The singers?"

"Who?"

"The girls who sang 'SWEET BETSY FROM PIKE'!" Ophie said, raising her voice.

"Oh, yah. Those singing girls," said Brittany. "They're the TV Girls."

"They're on TV?"

"Merry Morshak's dad sells cars. They sing the TV commercials."

"Really!" said Ophie. "Which one is Merry?"

"Merry is the one with the curly hair," Brittany said slowly. "Rachel Peacock is the one with the black."

"Merry and Rachel," Ophie murmured. She crossed her arms. "Well, they aren't very good," she said.

"Excuse me?" said a frowning girl. Ophie couldn't help but notice her teeth, which were covered with a ferocious set of braces. "What did you just say?"

"She said, 'Well, they aren't very good,'" Brittany confirmed. "That's what you said— huh, Peeler?"

"Yes," said Ophie, taking her voice down a notch, "that's what I said, but—"

"Oooh!" The girl with the braces gave her a metallic sneer before walking off. "I'm sure they'll be glad to hear that."

"That's Robin," said Brittany. "She tells on everyone."

"Uh-oh," said Ophie. "You don't think she'll tell those singer girls, do you?"

"She will," said Brittany.

Ophie wished she had kept her mouth shut. These girls were obviously the stars of the whole class. Just like she and Lizzy had been. Sort of. Mostly.

"Look there," said Brittany. "She's telling already."

Robin whispered in Merry Morshak's ear, and Merry's dimples disappeared. Rachel leaned in, and her mouth dropped open like a cartoon character's. Suddenly, all three of them were glaring directly at Ophie.

"What you gonna do?" Brittany asked.

Ophie started thinking. "Well," she said slowly, "I think I'm just going to pretend nothing ever happened."

"Huh?" said Brittany.

"Yeah! And then when I come back here in the morning, I'll pretend THAT'S my first day and I'll start all over. Get it?"

Brittany looked as if Ophie had pulled a rabbit out of a hat. "You can't do that."

"Well, that's what I'm gonna do."

Brittany stood there a long time. She was obviously impressed.

I'll just rewind, that's all, thought Ophie, *back to the start of the yellow brick road.*

Chapter Three

Ophie sat on the floor of her bedroom with her fists balled up against her eyes. She was making a picture in her head of Margaret Scott Elementary School, except it had gardens with bright flowers and a sun that never stopped shining. Onstage at the cafetorium with good friends Merry and Rachel, Ophie wore ruby red shoes. Her ruby red shoes . . . Her RUBY RED SHOES . . .

Bleh. Nothin'.

"Ophie?" Mrs. Peeler said. "Is everything okay?"

"Yes. Good. Just kinda resting," she said.

"You sure?" Callie had a bad night with bronchitis and was still fussing in her mother's arms.

Ophie didn't like to tell her mother everything she was thinking. Not anymore. "I'm sure," Ophie said, smiling weakly.

"You have company," her mother said.

"I do?"

"I think so. A couple girls are out there on the lawn."

Ophie followed her mother down the hall and cracked open the front door.

"Hey, Peeler."

There, wearing overalls and old tennis shoes, was big Brittany Borg with her skinny little sister, Tana.

"Oh. Hi," Ophie said, staring at the two of them standing there like mismatched totem poles.

"We're here to take you to our school," Brittany explained.

"Hello, girls!" Mrs. Peeler took the baby's hand and waved. "This is baby Callie!" Then she patted Ophie's head. "How nice, sweetie," she whispered. "Already, some new friends!"

Ophie slowly picked up her backpack and went outside to meet the Borg sisters. "So . . . where did we leave off?" she asked.

"You said you were going to make today your first day."

"That's right!" said Ophie. She covered her face with her hands, then dropped them. "Hello. I'm Ophie Peeler. Have we met?"

"You know we did," Brittany said.

"But we're supposed to pretend we haven't," Tana whispered.

Brittany crossed her arms. "Nope. I won't lie."

"Okay," Ophie said, feeling as if this conversation was already taking too much effort. "How about if we don't say it's my first day, then? What if we say it's my second first day, instead?"

Brittany considered. "Yah. That's good. I can do that," she said at last.

"So where did you used to go to school, Brittany?" Ophie continued.

"In the kitchen," said Brittany.

"What kitchen?" she asked Tana.

"Ours!" insisted Tana. "We really both went to school in our kitchen. Most of the time."

"Home school," Brittany said.

"Why did you stop?" asked Ophie.

"Too crowded," said Brittany.

"It's true!" said Tana. "Mama said Brittany was getting too big and too old to stay at home all day."

"Except we do go to Sunday school," said Brittany. "Every week."

"Hmm," Ophie said. "My school is always changing and I'm always on my way to somewhere else."

"At least you're not always with strangers. You have a sister!" said Tana.

"Yeah, but she's still too scrunched up and screamy to be much fun."

"She'll get bigger," Brittany said.

"I know," said Ophie. "Anyway, I never feel

like a stranger. I always think I'm more of a . . .
surprise magical visitor," she said, spreading
her hands like a fan as unmagical Margaret
Scott Elementary came into view.

★ ★ ★

On Ophie's second first day, Miss Fast gave a
writing assignment. Everyone was to write
haiku about the seasons. Ophie raised her hand.

"Miss Fast," she asked, "which seasons do
you want us to use?"

"Uh," said Miss Fast, "fall, winter, spring,
summer. The usual seasons."

"No, I KNOW that," said Ophie. "But do you
want the seasons you find, like, on Christmas
cards, or the seasons that they have down in
California, or the seasons here?"

"Hmm," said Miss Fast. "Well, I suppose I'll
leave that choice up to you."

Brittany Borg raised her hand. "We don't
have seasons on our Christmas cards, Miss
Fast. Ours just show Bethlehem."

"Then you just write about the seasons we
have here, Brittany," said Miss Fast.

"Here's an example of a winter haiku," said Miss Fast. "Remember, you have three lines and you have to count the syllables. Five syllables for the first line, seven syllables for the second line, and five syllables for the third line." She wrote on the board:

A hard winter snow. (5)
Frost covers the windowpanes. (7)
The fields are buried. (5)

"A haiku paints a picture, doesn't it?" Miss Fast smiled hopefully. Ophie looked around the room. All the kids were too busy counting on their fingers to look up. "Well, if there are no more questions," said the teacher, "why don't we start?"

Swetty and frightened! wrote Ophie. Five simple syllables. She was not sure why she chose them—they just came to her. She tapped her head with her pencil, then smiled.

Anaconda overhead!
Amazon winter!

Really good. She tried to think of another one.

Too dark to see things.
Spring inside a pyramid
with a dead mummy!

Hmmm. Don't like that one. Mummies are already dead, after all. She scratched out *dead* and wrote *mad,* instead.

I climb the mountain
straight up for a million feet.
I trip and FALL! Aaaaaaaahhhhhh!

Miss Fast might really like that one. Her last teacher had called that "thinking outside the box."

Ophie closed her eyes. *Water. The beach. Shark bites? Yes, those might work.* She thought of the Long Beach Aquarium, where her father had taken Ophie and Lizzy before they moved. And then she wrote: *Lizzy.*

Ophie stared at the word. Before she could stop it, a tear dripped down her nose and splotched her blue-lined tablet paper.

"Psst!!"

It was Brittany Borg. Ophie quickly wiped her cheek with the back of her hand and looked over.

"I HAVE KLEENEX!" she said in the world's loudest whisper.

Ophie shook her head.

"Hand your papers forward, please," said Miss Fast.

"But I'm not done!" said the index-card boy.

"Don't worry, Tyler," said Miss Fast. "I just want to check to see that you all understand the assignment. The final poems are going into our Open House folders."

The recess bell rang and the students sprang from their seats. Ophie barreled through the crowd to the door. Time to put her second first day plan into action. She shaded her eyes and began to search the playground for the TV Girls, when she felt a tap on the back.

"So, what you looking at?"

"I'm not looking AT anything, Brittany," Ophie said, busy scanning. "I'm looking FOR somebody. That Merry Morshak?"

"Over there," said Brittany. "In the corner."

Ophie squinted. "In that long line of girls?"

"Yah," Brittany said. "When Merry brings the Chinese jump rope, everybody wants to play. You should go play with Charlotte Camp. Like I do. Nobody stands in her line. Just some third graders."

Ophie followed Brittany's gaze. She recognized the redheaded girl from their class. And standing in Charlotte's very short line was Tana Borg.

"Okay. Let's go, Peeler," said Brittany.

Ophie shook her head. "No. I want to stand in Merry's line," she said.

"Huh?" said Brittany.

"I'm going over there right now," said Ophie. But every time she took a step left or right, Brittany took a step too.

"Brittany, *stand still!*" commanded Ophie, holding up her hand like a dog trainer.

Brittany obeyed and Ophie scooted past.

"It's late. You won't get a turn!" Brittany called after her.

After getting in line, Ophie found out that Brittany was right. Bored by the long wait,

Ophie asked Robin why it was that no one joined Charlotte's line.

"Because," said Robin, baring a mouth full of braces, "she's a *nose-picker*."

Ophie didn't know what to say.

"And her jump rope has cooties," continued the girl.

"Cooties?" Ophie said. "I don't believe in cooties. Did you ever think they might be a made-up thing?"

Robin looked indignant. "No," she said. "Where do you come from? Everyone knows cooties. They're *proven*."

"Then how come Brittany doesn't seem to care?" Ophie said. "About the cooties, I mean."

"Because Brittany," said Robin decisively, "is a cootie catcher." She paused. "Why? Is Brittany a *friend* of yours?"

"Actually, the reason I'm standing in this line is because I'm trying to make friends with those two up front. I'm a performer too. Plus, they kind of remind me of my old best friend. Back in California. Anyway, they're my type, I think."

Robin raised an eyebrow. "Merry Morshak and Rachel Peacock?"

"Yes!" said Ophie.

"Ha!" said Robin.

"What's so funny?" Ophie asked.

"Doubt they'll be interested," said Robin.

"Um, I really don't know what you're talking about," said Ophie.

"Think ya really do," said Robin.

Brrrriiiiinggggg! The recess bell.

"And that's strike two." Robin smiled.

Ophie lifted her chin. "I'm not counting," she said. *Besides, there's always lunch . . .*

Ophie spent the next hour in class ready to spring out of her chair. She scrambled to the cafeteria to survey the lunch line.

"The TV Girls eat brown-bag, like you," said Brittany. She was balancing a tray loaded with three Jell-O desserts. "But they're not here yet."

"Uh-huh. Thanks."

"They eat over at that table," Brittany continued.

"Okay," Ophie said.

"By the windows."

Ophie was starting to feel crowded again.

"Okay, then," she said. "I'll see you later." She started over to the TV Girls' table, but could still feel someone following closely behind her. Ophie had almost reached her destination, when, frustrated, she decided to suddenly STOP.

"Ooof!" Ophie felt the back of her shoe come off and the jab of an elbow.

"Smooth move!" crowed Tyler. "Three-girl pileup!"

A whole bunch of kids clapped.

Ophie wheeled around and found herself face-to-face with the TV Girls.

"What are you doing?" Merry Morshak demanded, rubbing her arm. Rachel was doubled over, holding her knee.

"Yikes! I'm sorry," Ophie said, wriggling her foot back into her shoe. "I really am." She hobbled to the corner table and sat down.

"That's *our* table," Rachel said to Merry. "She's sitting at our table!"

"I know you guys sit here," said Ophie. "That's why I came over."

Merry and Rachel remained standing.

"And I know what Robin told you!" Ophie said. "But I can explain!"

Merry and Rachel eyed her suspiciously, then reluctantly took their seats.

"Now, of course, you guys are mad," Ophie said quickly, "but you only heard PART of what I said, which is that when you sang, you didn't *sound* very good."

"So you DID say that?" Rachel asked.

"Yes, I said that. But I think it's probably because of the cafetorium. You know, the acoustics. I bet you probably sound a lot better on TV."

"We sound great on TV," Merry said calmly.

"I'm *sure* you do," Ophie agreed enthusiastically. "Because *I'm* a singer too. So I know all about these things."

"That so?" said Rachel.

"So if you ever need help rehearsing or staying on key or anything, I'll help you!

Maybe at recess? Next recess?"

Merry gasped.

"Or acting. I can help with that too. In my old schools, I was in every—"

"What *is* your name again?" asked Merry.

"Uh, Ophie. Ophie Peeler."

"Okay, Ophie Peeler. Guess what. Rachel and me have been best friends since preschool."

"Preschool," Rachel echoed.

"And we have been singing for my daddy on TV since we were in kindergarten!"

"That's five years," said Rachel.

"And I have never met anyone who said that me and Rachel can't sing. Everyone in town knows who we are. We were on Channel Thirteen's *Afternoon Cartoon Circus* . . ."

"Twice!" emphasized Rachel.

"And we had a float in the Rose Parade . . ." Merry continued.

"And don't forget the mayor's Prayer Breakfast!"

"And three appearances on Uncle Bob's *Drivetime* radio show . . ."

"Plus," said Rachel, "we modeled at the Bridesmaids' Expo . . ."

"Yes!" said Merry. "That was fun. Oh, Rachel. You looked so cute!"

"No," Rachel said, blushing, "you were the cutest!"

"But they made me wear yellow!" Merry made a face.

"You're cute in yellow!" insisted Rachel, poking Merry in the shoulder.

"Well, you're cute in pink and you know it!" Merry poked back.

"But I don't have your curls. I want your curls!" Rachel said in a fake baby's voice.

"Ha-ha-hee-hee!" The girls collapsed in giggles.

Ophie was trying to think of what to say next, when Merry and Rachel abruptly stopped laughing. At the same time they neatly opened their brown bags and each took out a sandwich. Merry looked up at Ophie as if she couldn't believe she was still there.

"We're going to eat lunch now," she said

simply, flashing her wide, bright smile. "See ya."

Ophie stood up. "I have a best friend too, you know." Her face felt hot. "A very wonderful friend. And she is cute too. More cute than both of you put together. And she can SING GREAT!" She pushed in her chair. "Her name is Lizzy Fannon, and this is the stupidest school I've ever been to!" She picked up her bag and started to walk off. But where to?

Brittany, who must have been watching the entire time, actually stood up on the lunch bench and waved her arms, making her over six feet tall. "Hey! I'm *here*, Peeler!" she shouted, as if she could possibly be over-looked.

Oh, my gosh.

Instead, Ophie walked as fast as she could out the door, down the hall, and into the only place she could think of. The bathroom.

She stepped into the last stall, locked the door, sat down, and reached into her bag. She took out her sandwich and bit off a corner.

Yuck. Spongy crust and that lonely *bathroom taste . . .*

Ophie stashed the sandwich and looked up. This stall had its own window way up high, and through the crinkly glass she saw tiny shadows. Ophie climbed up on the toilet to take a peek. Two chickadees were perched on the other side. She rested her hand against the glass, longing to be just that size, bunched up against the window all warm and feathery.

At the end of the day, Miss Fast passed back everyone's haikus. Maybe Miss Fast would make things better. Ophie imagined her teacher reading the poems, widening her eyes and saying out loud: *In all my years of teaching . . . !*

Ophie smiled expectantly at Miss Fast as she took the paper. She read the comments marked all over her page.

Because winter in the Amazon is hot?
Or because she's frightened?
This is a mummy poem. Please write
a haiku that describes Spring.

Fall) _This is NOT_ a poem about
Autumn.

[Lizzy] ???
Ophelia: You do know how to count
your syllables, but you need to stick
to the topic of the FOUR SEASONS.
Please try again. 😊
Miss Fast

Ophie read Miss Fast's words again. Her second first day was now officially worse than her first.

She put an X through the Amazon haiku and sat like a statue until the bell rang.

"Who cares?" she muttered as she walked home. "Who cares? How much longer will I have at Margaret Stupid Scott Elementary? Four months? Eight months? I can hold out for the next school!"

Ophie slowed when she reached the curb of her own house. What in the world was that noise? The place almost throbbed with the twang of guitars.

The sound grew louder as Ophie walked up

the path and followed the music to her front door. She pushed it open to a blast of song.

"Here comes the sun,
do-do-do-do
Here comes the sun, and I say
it's all right."

What sun? wondered Ophie. The sky today was as low and gray as always.

Mrs. Peeler carried baby Callie on her hip, held her little hand, and sang. They appeared to be . . . dancing?

"Ahem." Ophie felt strangely embarrassed.

"Ah! Welcome home!" said Ophie's mother.

"What's happening?" Ophie surveyed the room full of open boxes. Her mother must have been unpacking for hours.

"Callie and I are breaking the world record for setting up a household," Mrs. Peeler said. She bent her head until she and the baby touched noses. Callie, who had been fussing for weeks, opened her mouth and let out a deep-chested laugh. Mrs. Peeler laughed back, then buried her face in the baby's neck, making comical snorkeling sounds.

It seemed to Ophie as if she were viewing this scene from far away. Who were these silly, happy people?

"Do you know what I say?" Mrs. Peeler's eyes shone. "I say God bless the Mercury Athletic Shoe Corporation!" she proclaimed. "They've given your daddy an OFFICE job!"

Ophie felt her mom pull her close and cover the top of her head with kisses. "He has just three more weeks left on the road!"

Ophie couldn't breathe. She closed her eyes tight.

"Sweetie, do you know what this means?"

Ophie felt she was definitely going to cry.

"That's right, honey!" said Mrs. Peeler, starting to laugh again. "Oh, thank heavens! Home sweet home, at last. I'm going to completely unpack—for once. Isn't it wonderful? With any luck at all, we'll be staying for a long, long time . . ."

Ophie thought of all the miles and all the

faces; so many years spent skipping down so many yellow brick roads—and this is where it ends? Not in Oz. In *Oregon*.

The sunny song that had been playing came to an end, and Ophie could hear on the roof the distinct spatter of rain.

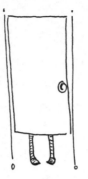

Chapter Four

When Ophie awoke, the first thing she saw was her mother standing over her and smiling. At first she started to smile back, but then she remembered the reason for her mother's smiling-since-yesterday smile.

"Good morning!" chirped her mom.

"Uh . . . morning," Ophie mumbled.

"Honey," said Mrs. Peeler, "I have a surprise for you." She smiled even wider and dangled a pair of red shoes above Ophie's head. "Thought you might have missed these."

"Oh. Thanks."

Ophie's mother raised her eyebrows. "What? Not into Dorothy anymore?"

"Nope."

"Hmmm." Mrs. Peeler sat on the edge of the bed and felt Ophie's forehead. "You okay?"

Ophie wished her mother wouldn't do that. Couldn't she see that Ophie's forehead had nothing to do with anything? "I'm not sick," Ophie said.

"Well, why don't you just tell me what's wrong?" Mrs. Peeler lifted Ophie's chin and stared into her eyes. "Please?"

Ophie stared back and didn't say a word. *Guess*, she thought.

Callie started to shriek, and Ophie's mother looked over her shoulder. "Oh, dear. She sounds cranky. Your poor sister's been so rashy lately." She stood up, hypnotized, Ophie thought, by the baby's every complaint.

"*Daddy* would've guessed," she said under her breath.

Mrs. Peeler stopped. "What would Daddy guess?" she asked.

"Nothing," said Ophie.

"Ophie," she said as the baby let out another screech, "let me take care of Callie and then we'll talk."

"But I don't want to talk," Ophie said after her mother left. "To you, or anyone." She sat with her arms folded for a moment, then yelled, "I QUIT!"

Ophie went down to the kitchen and turned on the TV. She dropped two Pop-Tarts into the toaster with a *ka-chunk*. Just as she looked up, she saw Merry Morshak and Rachel Peacock in the back of an old-fashioned convertible. On Channel 2!

Buy a Caddy from MY daddeeeee! Merry sang, bouncing her curls in perfect time to the music. Then Rachel put her head into the frame and joined her. *Don Morshak Cad-il-lac!* They ended with a wink and Merry's TV grin.

Ophie had been wrong about the acoustics thing. Merry and Rachel were just plain awful.

And it wasn't jealousy. If Lizzy were here, she would agree, Ophie was sure.

Ophie put on her coat and picked up her backpack. Once outside, she stuck her head into the front hall.

"Good-bye, Mom!" Ophie called.

Hearing no reply, she slammed the door.

She was hiding behind a bush when she spotted the Borg sisters hanging out by the stop sign. Why were they waiting for her? Just the thought of having to talk to Brittany seemed like work. They were too different. *She needs so much explaining . . .*

Even after the Borgs gave up and started moving, Ophie had to stay far behind so as not to be discovered. She was a whole block away when she heard the tardy bell ring.

"Oh, brother," she said. "Now I have to go to the office."

Ophie knew this because yesterday Tyler was tardy and had to go get a note before coming to class. On it, the school secretary had written: "LATE. LOOKING FOR BOOK. AGAIN." And

Miss Fast reminded Tyler in front of everyone that he should "organize his schoolwork" before going to sleep and not "disrupt the class" and be "more considerate of others' learning time."

Ophie knew she could not go through that this morning. And what would her note say? "MAD AT SMILING MOTHER. STUCK IN OREGON. HIDING FROM BRITTANY."

No. Maybe she could just sneak in at recess or something. She could say her mom's car broke down. Or she went to the dentist or . . .

Ophie slipped down the hall, rushing past the classroom doors until she got to the bathroom. She chose the same stall she sat in yesterday. After closing the silver latch and hanging her backpack on a hook, she felt strangely cozy, as if this were now her own little room.

After sitting awhile, she looked up and checked the window. The fluffy chickadees were still there. Ophie stood on the toilet to see them more closely. She put her nose against the glass and sang softly. "If happy little bluebirds fly beyond the rainbow, why oh why . . . ?"

The sound in the bathroom was nice. "I would not be just a nothin', sittin' full of stuffin'," she sang, "my heart all full of *paaain*!"

Then Ophie heard a creak. Over the top of the stall she saw the big bathroom door swing open. *Yikes!* She crouched and listened.

"I'll wait," said a girl. "But you should still hurry."

Ophie heard water turning off and on.

"Stop fooling around!" said the girl. "I bet you don't even have to go to the bathroom."

"Yes I do!"

Ophie thought the voices sounded pretty young. There was lots of banging. Doors opening and slamming?

"I'm going to tell!"

"No you won't!"

There was more scuffling until someone crashed against the outside of Ophie's stall. Hard.

"Ouch!"

"Whoa. This one's locked."

The door rattled, and Ophie stood as still as she could on her toilet perch.

"I don't see shoes," said one girl.

"Let me take a look."

Ophie watched as two little hands appeared on the floor. A pixie-haired girl who couldn't be more than six years old looked up, first curious—then terrified. Then she SCREAMED!

The girl outside the stall screamed too. The little short-haired girl bumped her head trying to escape. "There's a big hiding *girl* in there!"

"No!"

Both girls screamed together.

BAM-BAM-BAM!

"What's going on in there?" said a man.

Peeking over the stall, Ophie saw that the two little girls had opened the door and were now clinging to the custodian. "We saw her! There's a girl in there all sneaked up on the toilet!"

"This is Mr. Sam," boomed the custodian.

"Whoever is in that stall, you best come out right now!"

She climbed down and undid the latch. "It's just me," she said quietly. "Ophelia Peeler. From Miss Fast's room."

"What are you doing scaring little kids? You get back to class."

"Actually," said Ophie, "I never *went* to class."

"Hoo, boy," said Mr. Sam, as if he were deeply disappointed. He bent down to talk to the two little girls. "Do you kids think you can get back to kindergarten okay by yourselves?"

"But we didn't even get to go yet," said one girl.

The short-haired girl lowered her voice to a whisper. "She means *pee*."

"All righty, you two can go back in. But don't dawdle."

They nodded.

"Right now I'm going to have to take this girl to the principal."

Wide-eyed, the girls scrambled off. And without saying another word, Mr. Sam took Ophie by the elbow and guided her to the wooden bench inside the school office.

"This is Ophelia Peeler," Mr. Sam said to the school secretary. "She's supposed to be in Miss Fast's class. Instead, she's been hiding in the girls' restroom."

"Is that right?" said the secretary. "Thank you, Sam. I'll call Mrs. Dickerson."

Ophie sat on a bench, listening to the secretary talk all about her to the principal. She studied the top of her shoes with great concentration.

"You may go in now, Ophelia," the secretary said.

Ophie stood up quickly and was amazed by the tremble in her knees. She gave the door a little knock.

"COME IN!" said the principal.

Uh-oh. So loud.

The principal, Mrs. Dickerson, leaned forward on her large metal desk. Ophie noticed the half-glasses perched on the end of her nose and that the edges of her red-lipsticked mouth were turned way down.

"Miss Peeler," she began, "as you know, this is a school. Perhaps you will tell me what kind of education you hoped to get in the bathroom?"

Ophie covered her face. "I thought . . . I just can't explain it. Nobody understands," she said.

"My goodness," said Mrs. Dickerson.

"Nobody here anyway," whispered Ophie.

"Well, why don't you try me?" said Mrs. Dickerson. "I'm here."

Ophie shifted from foot to foot. That's what Mom said, thought Ophie, wondering if she should risk it.

"I'm all ears," said Mrs. Dickerson.

Ophie wrinkled her nose. "I don't know who to be anymore," she finally said.

"Really? Who did you used to be?"

"Um . . . Well, once I was Dorothy of Oz." Ophie thought Mrs. Dickerson might laugh, but she didn't. "I used to be almost exactly like

51

her," she continued. "Like, I traveled all around a million places and I had the red shoes and I could sing, which always made me happy. But now I'm not going anywhere and I don't think the shoes work anymore."

"And what about the singing?" asked Mrs. Dickerson.

Ophie noticed how Mrs. Dickerson leaned her cheek upon her hand as if she were per-fectly willing to listen.

"Before this school," Ophie replied, "I've always been an actor and a singer. I sing the rainbow song. You know . . ."

"The rainbow song? Hmmm," said Mrs. Dickerson. "Maybe I could hear it?" The prin-cipal leaned back in her chair.

"Really?" said Ophie.

Mrs. Dickerson nodded.

"Uh, okay," said Ophie. She felt her skin heating up and begin to prickle all over. She breathed in and out to calm herself, and looked up at the ceiling until she had the right feeling. Then she began with—

Some-where o-ver the rainbow,
way up high
There's a land that I heard of,
once in a lul-la-by . . .

As she sang, Ophie surprised herself. She got a lot of the little trills and catches just right. Troubles were sort of melting like lemon drops. She could almost feel herself floating off the floor as she sang the final words—

Why oh why can't I?

The silence afterward was good, weird, and seemed to last a long time.

"My, my," said Mrs. Dickerson at last. "Oh, my . . ."

Ophie looked at the principal. Were Mrs. Dickerson's eyes a little . . . wet?

"Sit down, Ophelia," she said. "Please."

Ophie sat and folded her hands in her lap.

"See this?" said Mrs. Dickerson, pointing to her own head. "What color would you say that my hair is?"

"I would say that it is gray," Ophie told her.

"Yes," said Mrs. Dickerson. "To you it is gray,

to Miss Fast it is gray, to my husband, to my children—my hair is gray. But you know what?"

"What?" said Ophie.

"I know that it is also a gorgeous, flaming red. Because just as you are also Dorothy of Oz, I am also the beautiful redheaded actress Rhonda Fleming. It's true . . . I have been Rhonda Fleming ever since I saw the film *Cry Danger!*"

"Uh-huh," said Ophie, feeling a little embarrassed. She had no clue who Rhonda Fleming was. But she got the idea.

"Now, I am not a crazy person," Mrs. Dickerson continued. "But I *know* I'm partly Rhonda Fleming, and now you know, but I'm certainly not going to show up at school with flame-red hair. Really, I think that would just ruin everything."

Ophie nodded in agreement. Just the thought of Mrs. Dickerson in flaming hair was *really* embarrassing.

"So here is what I do. I keep my Rhonda

Fleming in *my secret heart*." Mrs. Dickerson tapped her chest and gave Ophie a knowing look. "Do you know what I mean?"

"Maybe. I think."

"I don't ask much of her, don't advertise her. And most of the time, I'm perfectly glad to be your principal. But every once in a while, when I'm in the mood, Rhonda Fleming comes out."

Ophie thought for a moment. "Except she's not really a true secret anymore, is she? Because now I know too."

"You have a point, dear," conceded Mrs. Dickerson.

"But that's good. That's good!" said Ophie. "Because I'd rather not have a complete, total secret. It's better to have somebody to tell some things. You know?"

"Yes, I think I do," Mrs. Dickerson agreed.

"At my old school, I used to have a friend like that," Ophie said. "It was like everything I said, she knew just what I meant. And sometimes I knew what she meant even before she finished saying it. And sometimes she didn't have to say anything and I still knew. And she was the exact same with me."

"I can certainly understand that," said Mrs. Dickerson. "You are very easy to confide in. Why, look at me! I've known you for all of ten minutes, and already I've told you one of my deepest secrets."

Ophie felt her skin prickling and heating up again. But in a good way.

"Now, you see? There is really no reason for you to hide out in the bathroom. Dorothy is definitely still inside you. I just heard her singing. Wouldn't it be a shame for her to stop?"

"Singing?" Ophie asked, wondering if Mrs. Dickerson wanted another song.

"Well, yes. But not while Ophie Peeler is supposed to be in class."

Mrs. Dickerson looked down at her watch. "Oh. Getting late. If you go out right now and ask the secretary for a tardy note, you can join everyone for recess."

"Okay," said Ophie, a little sad that this meeting was over.

Mrs. Dickerson stood and walked to the door. Just before she opened it, she said, "I hope you have a nice day." And then she whispered in Ophie's ear: *"Dorothy . . ."*

Ophie smiled. "Thanks, Mrs.—*Rhonda Fleming!*" And as she walked out into the office, she held her hands to her chest. It had been a long time since she felt full of a bursting happiness, all the way to the bottom of her secret heart.

Chapter Five

All over the classroom on Monday morning, girls were finding purple envelopes in their desks.

Next to Ophie, a girl named Laura Poole had one—a see-through envelope with sparkly confetti inside. Ophie could see the confetti was shaped like ice skates, that the card was an invitation to Merry Morshak's birthday ice-skating party, and that it made a shiny, sparkly mess when you took the invitation out.

Ophie lifted the lid on her old scratched metal desk. She blinked. Nothing sparkly. Nothing purple.

All through social studies, Ophie stared at an ice skate confetti piece hanging from a strand of Laura's hair. She was pretty sure that Laura didn't know it was there; but Ophie decided that if she got an invitation to Merry Morshak's skating party, she'd make sure to dangle a piece of confetti in her own hair too.

During P.E., Ophie cornered Brittany Borg. "You get a purple envelope?" she whispered.

"Nah," said Brittany.

"Me neither." Ophie looked around. "Who else didn't get one?"

"None of the boys got one," said Brittany.

"Who else?" said Ophie.

"Oh, yeah. And Charlotte Camp."

"Where's Charlotte?" Ophie asked.

"She's over there on the bench." Brittany pointed. "Tying her shoe."

Ophie peered at the redheaded girl with the supposed cooties. She *was* crumpled over, but she wasn't tying her shoe. "Charlotte's *crying*, Brittany!" Ophie said.

Brittany narrowed her eyes. "Whoa. You're right."

Mrs. Beet blew on her whistle. "We're counting off for kickball, girls!" she yelled. "Line up against the wall!"

Ophie stared as Merry and Rachel huddled and whispered. Merry caught Ophie's gaze.

"Peeler!" she said, and motioned for Ophie to come over.

Birthday invitation, Ophie thought. She took her time walking. Better not to appear too eager.

"Stand next to me!" Merry commanded. Ophie, feeling somewhat confused, obeyed.

Meanwhile, Rachel Peacock grabbed Brittany Borg and hauled her over as well. Before Ophie knew it, both she and Brittany were standing shoulder to shoulder with the TV Girls!

"Count off by twos!" shouted Mrs. Beet. She pointed to the first girl.

One! Two! One! Two! One after another, the girls barked out their numbers.

"One!" said Merry.

"Two!" said Ophie.

"One!" said Rachel.

"Two!" said Brittany.

When the counting was done, Mrs. Beet tooted the whistle again. "Team ONE—you're in the field! Team TWO—you're up!"

Ophie watched as Merry and Rachel sauntered off with team one. *Merry just used me as a . . . a* place holder!

"Come on, Peeler," said Brittany.

Ophie gritted her teeth.

"We're team TWO!" Brittany said.

"I KNOW!" Ophie shouted.

Charlotte Camp was also on team two. Or she would have been, if her sniffling hadn't attracted the attention of the P.E. teacher. Ophie watched as Mrs. Beet walked over, patted Charlotte on the back, and spoke encouragingly while teams one and two took their places on the diamond. Brittany had just enough time to kick the ball deep into center field, when Mrs. Beet whistled again.

Tweeeeeeeeeeeet! "Stop the game!" she hollered. She gathered all the girls around the pitcher's mound.

"It has come to my attention," she said, "that certain girls in Miss Fast's class do not know the rules about *party invitations*!"

"SHE MEANS MERRY," said Brittany in her ear-piercing "whisper."

"We do not bring party invitations to school unless we invite *every* girl. Your parents should have received a notice to this effect at the beginning of school. The rules are *very clear*!"

Ophie glanced over at Merry Morshak, who looked like she just stepped barefoot on a bee.

"Party-invitation rule-breakers will be reported to Miss Fast! Consider this fair warning." Mrs. Beet put the whistle once more to her lips. *TWeeeeeeeet!* she trilled. "Continue play!"

How is Merry Supersmiley going to work her way out of this one? Ophie wondered.

At lunch, she found herself sitting with

Brittany Borg (or, rather, Brittany had sat with Ophie), eating Fritos, when Rachel Peacock stomped over to their table.

"Here!" She slapped down two purple envelopes and left.

"Guess we're invited," said Brittany.

Ophie looked down at her envelope. *Ophelia Peeler* was written in grown-up handwriting with purple ink. So, Merry had been *withholding* her invitation all along.

"I don't even want to go to this thing now," said Ophie.

"But I've never ice-skated before," said Brittany.

"That isn't the point," said Ophie.

Brittany peered closely at the envelope. "It isn't?"

"No, Brittany. It isn't."

Ophie started imagining all sorts of spectacular gifts. It'd be great to give Merry something intimidating! She pictured her standing on a stepladder unwrapping a wide-screen TV, *FROM OPHIE PEELER* written on the gift tag.

"I still want to go," said Brittany. "For the skating."

"Mmm-hm," said Ophie.

"But I don't know about the present," said Brittany.

"Why's that?" said Ophie, munching.

"Because she already has everything," continued Brittany. "And our family is on a budget."

Ophie brightened. "You know, if we put our money together, we could get her something fantastic!"

"But you don't like her," Brittany said.

"I know! And she doesn't like us. So, we got to show her that she's a dope for hating us." Ophie paused. *Did I just make Brittany Borg and me into an US?*

"Oh," Brittany said. "All I got is three dollars and thirty cents. My mom makes us use our own allowance for presents."

"Well, my mom usually gives me about fifteen dollars for things like this," Ophie said. "Plus I have some quarters. So we could have, maybe, twenty dollars."

Brittany crossed her arms. "That's too much."

"Listen," Ophie said, "the only way I'll go is if we can show up with something great."

Brittany finally agreed to let Ophie do the shopping. That evening she searched the Internet looking at toy stores and electronics and sites that sold girl stuff. After hours of looking at everything from computer games to ladies' shavers, the choice was obvious: She was going to get Merry a karaoke machine.

Yes, a karaoke machine! And she would write her a personal birthday song too! Which she would sing into a microphone at the party.

It was a great idea, but the only problem was . . . the price. The cheapest one Ophie could find was on sale for $34.99. The others were more than twice that. So she got on the phone with ToysUSA to do some bargain hunting.

The woman laughed. "No, honey, we have nothing like that for twenty dollars."

Ophie called every kids' store in the shopping mall. She was just about to give up when she decided to call a store called Biggs Discount.

The kids' department there did have something they called "Kitty Karaoke." For nineteen dollars! And it came with its own tapes.

"Perfect!" Ophie said. She couldn't believe her luck—until her mother brought the thing home a few days later.

"Ophie," her mother warned, "don't get your hopes up." She held up a very small bag.

"Is that it?"

Ophie's mother lifted the karaoke machine from the sack.

It was a plastic kitty cat's head that ran on six D batteries and had headphones that didn't quite reach Ophie's ears. Even when Ophie turned the volume up all the way, she could barely hear the tune—a jingly instrumental version of "The Itsy-Bitsy Spider."

"Ish," Ophie said.

"Want me to take it back?" asked Mrs. Peeler.

"I don't know. Let me think." She looked down the list of possible songs on tape number two, which featured a patriotic theme. *"Yankee Doodle"? "This Land is Your Land"?*

"I can make it work," Ophie said. "I'll keep it."

"That's my resourceful girl!" Mrs. Peeler beamed.

"Uh, thanks," Ophie replied.

★ ★ ★

Ophie spent days writing and practicing her song for Merry. Feeling some pre-party jitters, she was actually relieved to see Brittany in the ice rink's parking lot. "Hey look!" said Ophie. She showed Brittany the box wrapped in paper hand-painted with musical notes and a matching card in a huge manila envelope.

"You did good," said Brittany.

"Thanks! I did, didn't I?" Ophie said. "Come on, let's go inside."

It was easy to spot the kids who were there for Merry's party. They were huddled at the front desk, kicking off their shoes and exchanging them for skates. Behind the plate-glass window, some girls were already gliding around the rink.

"Where's Charlotte?" Ophie asked.

"Don't know," said Brittany.

"Probably too embarrassed to show up after all that sobbing," Ophie said.

"This way, ladies!" said a beautiful brunette woman in a white ski coat. She had big white teeth and a giant diamond ring. It was the same lady who videotaped Merry singing "Sweet Betsy from Pike."

"Hello, you two. I'm Merry's mother," she said, taking the gift and card from Ophie. Mrs. Morshak looked down at the gift, batted her eyes a few times, and said, "Oh, *my*!" Finally, she led them to the front desk for skates.

Ophie waited while Brittany explained her needs to the teenage counter clerk.

"I have flat feet," she said.

"Okay," said the counter girl.

"And I have a high instep," she continued.

"Really?" said the girl, curling her lip.

"They're also wide," said Brittany.

"Interesting," said the clerk. "What's your size?"

"Seven and a half," said Brittany.

Ophie sighed.

The clerk bent down, picked up a pair of size 7½ skates, and thrust them at Brittany. "Next!" she said.

"Size four," said Ophie. As the counter clerk searched, Ophie absentmindedly looked over her shoulder out at the rink. There was Merry Morshak in a bright blue velvet skating dress with a hood trimmed in . . . silver imitation fur!

The sound system was playing *Beauty and the Beast*. ("Song as old as time . . .") Merry skated in wide circles holding out her arms. Then she tucked in her knee and started spinning so fast, Ophie couldn't tell her back from her front. Merry was a much better skater than she was a singer.

"Oh, she's just so so beautiful, I think," said Laura Poole, the girl with confetti in her hair.

"Yeah," Ophie had to agree.

"And graceful," Laura continued. "And such a good singer."

"Well, she *is* graceful, that's for sure," Ophie said diplomatically.

Laura looked into Ophie's face and squinted. "Hey," she said, "don't I know you from some-place?"

"Yes. My name is Ophie. I'm in Miss Fast's class."

"Really?" she said.

"I sit right behind you," Ophie said, feeling a little insulted.

"You do?"

"And I sit on the side of you," chimed in Brittany. "C'mon, Peeler. You ready?"

"And who's Peeler?" Laura asked.

"ME!" Ophie said "See you on the rink."

When Ophie got on the ice, the only way she could keep her feet from slipping out from under her was to cling to the edge of the rink. Brittany was having better luck.

"I don't tip over," she said. "Hang on to my arm."

Ophie hung on desperately. "Just go straight," she said. "I can't turn!"

"Move your feet like this," said Brittany. She left Ophie wobbling and showed her how to spread her feet apart and pull them back together over the ice. "It isn't hard at all."

Trembling, Ophie went pigeon-toed and stuck out her behind. She started moving backward!

"Hey, how do you do that?" said Brittany. She stuck out her rear end and did the pigeon-toed move too. Pretty soon, they were both skating backward, *very slowly*, together.

"At least I'm not falling down," said Ophie. But skating backward was very hard on her ankles. And everywhere she went, so did Brittany.

Rachel sailed by with a grin on her face. She said over her shoulder, "You two look like a couple of garbage trucks backing up!" Every time Robin passed them, she went: "BEEP-BEEP-BEEP-BEEP!"

"That's the sound of a garbage truck," Brittany explained.

"Hey, that's Laura," said Ophie. "Hi there, Laura!"

But Laura, looking aghast at Ophie, skated

around them in a circle before speeding off.

"Bet she remembers you now," Brittany said.

Just then Merry's mother called them over for hot cocoa.

Finally, thought Ophie.

"Shall we open presents now, darling?" Mrs. Morshak asked Merry.

"I want to skate some more!" said Merry.

"Gifts first, sweetheart. A nice little break for everyone, hmmm?"

The corner of the lobby was jam-packed with colorfully-wrapped presents. Mrs. Morshak pulled up a chair for Merry before the giant pile and began videotaping.

"Okay, honey," she said. "Pick one up! That's it. Now give me that knockout smile and read the card."

Mrs. Morshak handed Merry present after present. The girls ooohed and ahhed at the opening of every gift, and Merry turned on her trademark grin with every thank you.

Ophie scooted to the front as soon as she

saw Merry pick up her present. Brittany muscled her way in next to Ophie and stood with her hands on her hips. "I want to watch you," she said.

Merry opened the envelope and pulled out the card that—*ploop!*—unfolded like a road map to her knees. *"Press the button on the machine for your musical birthday card . . . To be sung to the tune of 'America the Beautiful'?"* She gave Mrs. Morshak a look of warning. "I'm *not* singing, Mother!"

"Oh, *you* don't have to—" began Ophie.

"But Merrykins," interrupted Mrs. Morshak, "you're a singer! It would be such a treat."

"Yes!" squealed Rachel.

"Sing! Sing! Sing!" the girls cheered.

Ophie stood frozen as Merry pretended to be shy while the girls kept begging. "First let me turn on this . . . *thing*," she said. She kept pressing the wrong buttons on the kitty's head.

Ophie stepped forward. "It's *this* one," she said, pressing firmly. The introduction started, very softly.

"Doesn't this go any louder?" Merry asked nobody in particular.

"No," Ophie said.

"Testing. Testing," she said. "At least the microphone works. Let's try it again, Peeler." She motioned for Ophie to press the button.

I'm supposed to sing it to you! Ophie wanted to say. But she pushed Play instead.

Merry tapped out the beat, and then began:
"When you were born ten years ago
I bet your mom was glad.
But no one could be happier
than Merry Morshak's dad!
His Cadillacs were all for sale
But no one came to buy.
He thought the family would be poor.
It made him want to cryyyy!"

You could hardly tell it was "America the Beautiful," or that it rhymed, perfectly.

"Then Merry looked up from her crib
and said Dad don't be blue!

'Cuz me and my best preschool friend
will sell them all for you!
He dressed them up in pretty clothes
and put them in a car.
They sang on TV day and night,
Now Merry is a STAR!

"The years have passed and many cars
of Morshaks have been sold.
They are so rich, their toilet seats
are made of solid gold!
They're filling up their swimming pool
with diamonds, jewels, and pearls!
Hip hip hooray, her parents say,
God bless our little girl!"

The girls were laughing and cheering. Mrs.
Morshak threw her arms around Merry and
gave her a big kiss. Merry bowed and smiled
her toothpaste smile. Mrs. Morshak curtsied,
and quickly handed Merry another present.

Ophie backed out of the way and stood sim-
mering behind that crowd of girls.

"Hey, Peeler," Brittany said. "I thought you were going to sing."

"I was supposed to," Ophie whispered. "And *I* would have done a good job."

And that's when it finally hit her: As long as Merry had ice skates and fake fur and TV commercials, she could be as crummy as anything. Merry ruled the stage at school. And everywhere else. She just did.

And I just . . . don't.

Chapter Six

Over the next few weeks, Brittany and Tana Borg waited for Ophie every morning on the walk to school. And Ophie gave up and started watching for them too. She wasn't sure exactly why. Conversations with Brittany were still hard to get started.

"So what's going on?" Ophie would ask.

"We're waiting for you," Brittany would say.

"What else?" said Ophie.

"That's all," Brittany said.

Ophie kept trying. "Well, then," she said, racking her brains, "let me ask you something my friend Lizzy asked me once: If you had no other choice—no choice or else they'd kill you—what would you rather do? Sleep out in the middle of the woods all night in just a sleeping bag? Or drive your mom's car on the freeway?"

Tana made up her mind pretty quickly. "Stay overnight in the woods!" she said. "Because I know if I drove on the freeway, I'd get creamed for sure."

But Brittany was quiet. After a whole day of thinking, she revealed her answer on the way home.

"Okay, I'm thinking that I'd probably rather drive. IF I can stay on the side of the freeway and go real slow," said Brittany. "Also, if a cop chases me, I'd be glad, because then I could stop and tell him that someone is making me drive on the freeway or else they'll kill me. And then he could let me ride in his car and we could catch that person and put them in the prison, where he couldn't bother kids ever again."

Then one morning when Ophie was too tired

from the baby keeping both her and her mother awake half the night, Tana decided to take over the conversation.

"Brittany has a boyfriend," she announced.

"No way," said Ophie.

"Way. She really really has a boyfriend."

"You do?" Ophie asked.

"Yah. From church," said Brittany.

Ophie studied Brittany for signs of a romantic glow. "When you say BOYFRIEND," said Ophie, "I mean, are you in love?"

"Yes," said Brittany.

"Are you going steady?"

"No," said Brittany. "But I've known him since third grade. Anyhow, he gave me this pinkie ring."

"Let me see!" said Ophie. She grabbed Brittany's hand. She had noticed the ring before—an adjustable gold band with a chip of red diamond. "You're not kidding! Oh, Brittany! You DO have a boyfriend!"

Brittany gave her a puzzled look. "Like I said."

"What's his name and how old is he?" Ophie asked, heat rising to her cheeks.

"His name's Troy and he's eleven."

"Oh, Brittany," gasped Ophie, "if your parents say yes, you can marry him in Arkansas in THREE YEARS! Is he cute?"

"He's big for his age!" volunteered Tana. "His parents took him to the doctor to make sure he was normal."

"Why did you two wait so long to tell me about this? This is so . . . It's the best thing that's happened so far, don't you think?"

"Yes," said Brittany.

"Do you write about him in your diary?"

"Brittany doesn't have a diary," said Tana.

"But you *have* to have a diary!" Ophie thought that if she had a boyfriend, she would lie on her bed and write in a diary with a pink feather pen.

"He e-mails me," said Brittany.

"You e-mail him back?"

"Mmm-hm," said Brittany.

For the rest of the day, Ophie tried to get

Brittany to tell her more about Troy. "Just think," she said at recess, "you're a girl with a *boyfriend*!" And at lunch, "What do you think Troy is thinking about *right now*?" And on the way home, "So, do you miss Troy? I'll bet you really miss him."

But Brittany wouldn't say! And here she was, watching the TV Girls on the other side of the street, knowing that her group could have real, live boyfriend talk—yet no boyfriend conversations were taking place.

"Let's e-mail him!" Ophie said.

Brittany walked forward single-mindedly.

"Oh, please, please! Or just let me watch you e-mail him!"

Brittany stared straight ahead. "I don't e-mail him until after supper."

"Why?" Ophie asked.

Tana raised her hand and bounced up and down. "I know! I know!" she said. "Because that's what they e-mail each other about. They tell what they had for supper."

"That's it?" Ophie said.

Brittany Borg stopped in her tracks. "THAT'S IT!" she said.

Ophie jumped. "Well, you don't have to get mad," she said, feeling taken aback.

"That's the way we always do it and I don't want to do anything different," said Brittany.

"All right!" said Ophie.

"See you tomorrow, Peeler," Brittany said.

Who knew that Brittany could be so touchy? Ophie tried to imagine herself in Brittany's place. She pictured herself staring into the computer screen, typing *MEAT. MASHED POTATOES. GREEN SALAD. MILK. OKAY THAT'S ALL GOOD NIGHT*. Maybe Brittany just couldn't think of anything else to say. She wasn't the greatest talker.

Well, Ophie had an idea . . .

Dear Troy,

So LoNELY 4 U. I did not have the heart to even touch the soup that LIZEE our maid served us tonight. Miss Brittany you did not touch the soup! she said with such disappointment. But all I could do was stare into the candles and remember you and me together last sunday at church school.

My most trusted friend tells me that we can go to Arkansas in 3 years to be married. I do not dare ask mama and papa. But LIZEE who was once in love but lost her boyfriend because her dad did not like him would probably be soft hearted. I could be smuggeled out in her trunk and we could meet at the train station.

Too bad we will have to wait 3 whole years. You must here my sighs all the way over in your neighborhood. How I wish I could give you a big kiss. Write back when you get this.

xoxoxo,

Brittany

Now THAT was an e-mail about dinner, and then some! Ophie called Brittany's house and Tana answered the phone.

"I have something I want to e-mail Brittany," said Ophie. "You can look at it too if you want!"

"Oh, goody!" said Tana.

"In fact, you might look it over first and tell

me what you think about it. I don't want Brittany to get mad," said Ophie.

"Oh, I will!" said Tana.

Ophie wrote down the e-mail address Tana gave her and immediately sent the romantic letter to the Borgs. The phone rang again in ten minutes.

"I love the letter, Ophie," said Tana. "It's like a storybook."

"Yep," said Ophie. "That's what I was trying to do."

"I wonder what Troy will think."

"Ha!" said Ophie. "I don't think that Brittany would ever actually send that to Troy! I just wanted to give her some ideas, you know, in case she ever wants to write about something besides dinner. It was kind of a joke."

"Uh-oh," said Tana.

"Uh-oh what?"

"I sent it. Ophie, I sent it! To Troy. I thought that's what you wanted, to do something nice for Brittany. And I loved that letter and oh, I'm so sorry."

"Aye, Chihuahua," Ophie said.

After mulling it over, Tana added, "Hey, maybe he won't read it at all?"

"Or maybe he'll know it's a joke. Or something," said Ophie.

Finally, both girls decided it might be a good idea just to sit tight and see what happened.

The next morning, Ophie ran to meet Brittany and Tana.

"Hello!" Ophie waved. Her heart was bumping.

"Hey there, Peeler," said Brittany.

This was what Brittany said every morning. This was good. But then she noticed that Tana was hiding behind her sister and giving Ophie a panicky, eye-bulging look!

"How's it going?" Ophie asked.

"Okay," said Brittany.

"That's good," said Ophie, as Tana shook her head and pantomimed tearing out her hair.

As soon as they got to school, Tana said to Ophie, "I've got to go to the bathroom. Do *you* got to go to the bathroom?" She nudged Ophie in the ribs.

"I don't gotta go," said Brittany, who wasn't paying much attention.

"Well, *I* sure do," said Ophie.

Ophie and Tana ducked into the girls' room. "I think we did something really bad!" said Tana. "Last night Brittany got on the computer and told Troy what she had for supper and . . ."

"What?" said Ophie.

"He didn't mail her back! He *always* mails her back."

"Maybe he was gone?"

"He's *never* gone! And Brittany kept on checking all night until bedtime, and she checked this morning, and she feels real bad."

"How can you tell?" asked Ophie.

"Because she's my sister!" said Tana. "Oh, what can we *do*, Ophie?"

Ophie looked at Tana's worried little face. "We could try to explain. We could tell Troy it was just a joke. We can send him another e-mail!"

"I'm not sending anything. Ever."

"Then I'll send it. Give me Troy's address, and I'll make it better. I promise."

"Thank you," said Tana.

"Okay. But now you're going to have to let go of my arm," said Ophie.

"Oops," Tana said.

Imagine having a sister care about you like that, thought Ophie as she watched Tana walk away. She tried to think of the bellowing, scrunched-up Callie as her friend. It would be so nice to see her turn into . . . not a Lizzy replacement; maybe a Lizzy runner-up? But the baby just wasn't *ripe* enough yet for Ophie to tell if that could happen.

At home, Ophie sent Troy an e-mail.

Dear Troy:
I am Brittany's friend and I am the one who sent you the note about getting married and being in love. I did it for a joke. I hope you are not mad at Brittany. It was not her idea at all. Tana sent it by accident.
Ophie Peeler

But the next day, when she met up with the Borg sisters, Tana was just as worried.

"What's up?" said Ophie.

"Nothing," said Brittany.

"I have to go to the bathroom," said Tana, shooting Ophie a doomed look, *"right when I get to school!"* And then Ophie felt nudged in the side. Hard.

Once safely inside the third bathroom stall, Ophie asked Tana, "What's wrong?"

"Did you send Troy the note?" asked Tana.

"Yes. I told him that Brittany didn't know anything about it."

"Well, he still isn't mailing her back. And she still doesn't know why. And now I don't know why! So what do we do now?" Tana asked.

"If he doesn't write, we're just going to have to wait until Sunday to find out," said Ophie. "Promise me something, Tana. When we meet in the morning, hold up one finger if Troy hasn't mailed Brittany yet. And if he has mailed her, hold up two fingers. Got it?"

"Yes," said Tana. "Good idea. 'Cuz I really

don't have to go to the bathroom every morning."

And although Tana held up one finger for the rest of the week, Brittany didn't seem much changed at all.

On Sunday, when the phone didn't ring, Ophie finally decided to call Tana herself.

"Hello, Tana?"

"Oh, Ophie," said Tana. "Ophie, Ophie, Ophie . . . It was terrible. *Soooo* bad."

"It can't be that bad . . . *can it?*"

"Troy Bachtman's mother got the Lizee note, and she told Troy he couldn't write Brittany anymore because it had *marriage* and *kissing*! Then she told Brittany that she had to stop e-mailing Troy about dinner, even though Brittany didn't write the note!"

"But I confessed! It's not Brittany's fault!"

"I know. But Mrs. Bachtman said, just who is this friend of yours? And Brittany said, this new girl from California. And Mrs. Bachtman didn't like *that* at all. And then she said she was very 'concerned' because she thought you were . . ."

Tana paused. "She said you were a 'very *aggressive* little girl.'"

"What?" Ophie took the news like a sock to the stomach. Mrs. Bachtman didn't even know her. "I thought aggressive means you like to punch people," said Ophie.

"I dunno," said Tana. "But Brittany is so mad at me, she is hiding in the RV in the driveway."

"I'm coming over," Ophie said. "Right now!"

Tana was waiting for her in the driveway. She pointed to the RV's metal door. "Brittany's in there," she said.

Ophie tried the handle. It was locked. She banged on the door.

"Nobody home!" said Brittany.

"Somebody has to be home to say 'nobody home,'" Ophie shouted. "Please, please let me in!"

"Nobody home!"

"If you think she's going to open that door," said Tana, "you're wrong. I'm just gonna have to tell my mom. And then my mom will find out about Mrs. Bachtman and then *I'll* be in trouble too."

Ophie thought. "Tana, just how mean *is* Mrs. Batman?" she asked.

"It's Mrs. BACHT-man," said Tana. "She isn't really mean. But she is very strict."

"Is she scary?"

"Hmm. I would say she's scary when she's mad."

Ophie stood straighter. "Do you have her phone number?" she said, as calmly as she could.

Tana's jaw dropped.

"I will call her and tell her I'm not aggressive. Because I'm NOT!" said Ophie. "And that this is all my fault."

"And, a little my fault too," said Tana.

True, thought Ophie.

Tana took Ophie upstairs to the phone in her parents' bedroom. She got out the church directory and Ophie bravely began to dial, when she realized that her mouth was completely dry. She hung up.

"Oh, boy," she rasped. "I'm going to need some water."

Tana fetched a cup of water from the bathroom and Ophie downed it. She swallowed hard and dialed again. "Mrs. Bachtman? Hello, Mrs. Bachtman, ma'am?"

Tana covered her eyes with her hands and pretended to scream silently.

"Yes. I'm Ophelia Peeler. Um, Brittany's friend? . . . Uh-huh. That's right, I am from California." *What's wrong with being from California?* Ophie had to wonder.

"Yes. I'm just calling to say I am very sorry about that e-mail and that Brittany didn't know. . . . No, she really didn't."

"Is she super-mad?" Tana whispered.

Ophie plugged her free ear. "No. I don't really do kissing. It was pretend. And I am *positive* that Brittany doesn't do kissing. I'm just sorry that all this happened. So, so sorry."

Tana moved in closer to the phone and tried to listen.

"No, no! I have plenty of supervision. And

Brittany has *tons* of supervision! Even though she doesn't need it. She always does the right thing all by herself."

Ophie was relieved to hear a change in Mrs. Bachtman's tone. She smiled and waved a hand at Tana so she'd know.

"Okay! Yes, thank you. Thank you very much, Mrs. Bachtman!" Ophie hung up the phone.

"What? Tell me!" said Tana.

"I fixed it! She believes me!"

"Let's go tell Brittany!" squealed Tana.

Both Ophie and Tana beat on the trailer door.

"Nobody home," said Brittany.

"Ophie called Troy's mom!" yelled Tana. "Everything is okay! You can come out now!"

The metal door opened a crack.

"I told Mrs. Bachtman it wasn't your fault," said Ophie. "And she said you can e-mail Troy—as long as it's just once a day."

Brittany poked her head out. "You sure?" she asked.

"Yes!" exclaimed Ophie. "I fixed it."

Brittany stepped out of the trailer. She inhaled and looked up at the cloudy sky.

Ophie was surprised at how glad she was to see Brittany back to her old self again. "So you want to mail him now?" she asked, careful not to sound too pushy.

"Nope," said Brittany, almost smiling. "Gonna wait," she said, resting her hands on her hips, "until after spaghetti!"

Chapter Seven

Ophie put on her rain jacket, pulled up her hood, and ran to meet the Borg sisters, who were also wearing rain jackets.

"Don't you guys get tired of wearing rain stuff all the time?" she asked.

"No, because we got reversibles," said Brittany.

"One side red, the other side plaid," said Tana. "We mix it up."

"Well, I'm going to go totally cuckoo if the sun doesn't come out soon," Ophie said to Brittany. "*Does* the sun ever come out?"

"Yah," said Brittany. "When it stops raining."

"We don't have much sun until May," said Tana. "I know that because it's my birthday month and I always have sun and good luck!"

"If we always have to be indoors, I wish we at least had our own place," said Ophie. "That would be good. Then maybe we could have a club."

"A club!" said Tana. "Let's have a club!"

"We could have it in the RV," said Brittany. "As long as we put everything back when we're done."

"Let's have our first meeting TODAY!" said Tana. "After school!"

"Yes!" said Ophie. "And everyone's job today is to think up what the club is about."

"What the club is about?" repeated Brittany.

Ophie couldn't understand why Brittany always had to think so hard. "It's really very simple," she explained. "Just think of some things that you know how to do! Stuff we can do at our meetings. And think of, maybe, what we'll name the club. Things like that."

* * *

Ophie had a secret hope that maybe, if she worked at it over time, Brittany could be taught to be a little more Lizzy-like. For now, while other students were called to the board to do long division, Ophie pictured herself with a gavel, bringing the club meeting to order with a bang.

Ophie continued daydreaming until Merry Morshak's name was called. She watched as Merry took the chalk from Miss Fast matter-of-factly, turned her back on the class, and worked on the problem with a machine-like efficiency. Ophie stared at Merry's perfect hair bow and felt a pang. She imagined Mrs. Morshak fluffing the ribbon as her daughter yawned, worrying about how Merry would look from the back while doing long division. How did Merry get everyone to make such a fuss over her?

What's more, if Merry wore a hair bow, Rachel knew to wear one too. And Ophie knew that within a few weeks, even people like Charlotte Camp would show up wearing bows.

It seemed that everyone knew that it was cool to do the thing that Merry did. Everyone except Brittany Borg.

"Well, that's one thing about us," said Ophie on the way home. "In our club, we don't have to do everything the same."

"Is that what our club can be about?" asked Tana.

"Good idea!" said Ophie.

Rain started spattering in big drops. The girls broke into a run, holding the tops of their hoods up to keep dry until they reached and rattled open the RV door.

Ophie gasped as she stepped inside. "Oh, how cute!" There was a nook with benches at the kitchen end of the trailer. And windows with curtains! And a microwave! It was like having their own little house. Even the rain clattering off the metal roof just made the clubhouse seem homier. "This'll be great! I call this meeting to order right now!" She banged the table with a fist.

"Okay," said Brittany. "First give me your

Weekly Reader. I know what I'm going to do for our club."

"You're not going to read us the *Weekly Reader,* are you?" asked Ophie.

"Nah! I already read it." Brittany took out her own paper from her pack and began to fold it quickly and neatly. In no time, she had a hat. She put it on her head.

"Can you make . . . anything else?" Ophie asked.

"I know how to make a boat, and I know how to make a hat," said Brittany.

"Make a boat!" said Tana.

"The boat *is* a hat," said Brittany.

"Well, then, make us all hats," sighed Ophie, digging in her backpack. She pulled out some markers and took a hat from Brittany. On it she wrote in red letters: *Dorothy of Oz.* "This is who I'm going to be today! See? It's the Be-Whoever-You-Want Club!"

"Me!" said Tana. She took a hat from Brittany and grabbed a blue marker. *Dorthy of Oz,* she wrote.

"But *I'm* Dorothy!" said Ophie.

"Isn't this the Be-Whoever-You-Want Club?" Tana asked.

"Yes," confirmed Ophie, "it is."

"Then we can both be her!" Tana said.

Brittany grabbed a brown marker and printed on her own hat in big letters: *EMT.* "That stands for Emergency Medical Technician," Brittany said. "Okay, who's sick?"

"I'm not," said Ophie/Dorothy.

"Me neither," said Tana/Dorothy.

Brittany frowned.

All three girls sat looking at each other for a while.

"You guys sick yet?" asked the EMT.

Ophie/Dorothy didn't really want to be sick. But she was starting to realize that if someone didn't get sick quickly, this was going to be the most boring club ever. Ophie stood up and put her hand to her forehead. "I'm . . . dizzy!" she announced, then collapsed on the trailer floor.

"Me too!" said Tana/Dorothy, who rolled off her chair and collapsed next to Ophie.

"All right!" said the EMT triumphantly. She knelt down and removed the paper hats from the fallen Dorothys' heads and put them over their faces. "Oxygen masks," she said. "Breathe deep. I gotta drive."

The EMT took the wheel of the RV and made loud siren noises. "Hold on!" she said, violently steering left and right.

It became clear that Brittany was way too serious about being an EMT. Anytime one of the Dorothys tried to stand up, she made her lie back down so she could thump on her and do CPR. "Cardiopulmonary Resuscitation," Brittany explained. "It's to get your heart restarted."

"Brittany," said Ophie, after an extra-thorough pounding, "I was thinking . . ."

"Me too," said Tana, rubbing her ribs.

"What?" said Brittany, her paper hat askew.

"I was thinking that maybe our club could be more about acting. You know, acting like certain people."

"That's what I'm doing," said Brittany.

"Yeah, you are," said Ophie. "But all me and Tana get to do is be sick. And there's no story to that, you know?"

"Oh," said Brittany.

"See, like with my friend Lizzy, we would just bounce things around. So I was thinking that in our club, I would have an idea, and I'd throw it to you, and you'd throw it to Tana."

"Throw?" said Brittany.

"I want to rethink the club," Ophie said.

"What do you mean?" Brittany asked.

"Let's give it a week. We'll think and think. And maybe we'll come up with something better."

"Can we still have hats?" said Brittany, looking as if this might be important to her.

"Uh, sure," Ophie said.

Ophie reconsidered whether you could even have a club with someone like Brittany. Especially if the theme had anything to do with acting or pretending. When you bounced her an idea, she caught it all right. But then Brittany tucked it under her arm for keeps.

She wasn't a bouncer-backer. Would she ever be?

A whole week later—on club day—Brittany was still excited about the old club. She kept folding miniature hats out of scrap paper at her desk. She loved pretending to be an EMT! Ophie, on the other hand, was not looking forward to getting thumped again.

With only thirty minutes of school left, Ophie was watching the minute hand on the clock going ka-chunk in slow motion, when she heard someone in the back of the room cry, "Miss Fast!"

Ophie looked back. It was Rachel Peacock, looking terrified. Next to her sat Merry Morshak with her hands clapped to her forehead.

"What's wrong?" asked Miss Fast.

"*Unnnnhhhh,*" groaned Merry.

"Please help her!" said Rachel.

Miss Fast hurried to Merry's desk and knelt by her side.

"I see colors," Merry gasped. She held her

head tighter. "It hurts, it hurts!"

"She gets migraine headaches," Rachel explained. "They're really bad."

Ophie watched as Miss Fast gently guided Merry from her chair. "We'll go to the nurse," she said. "Class, please read silently while we're gone."

"I can't see!" squealed Merry, stretching out her arms.

"Just lean on me, dear," said Miss Fast, opening the door.

"I can't SEE!" Merry shrieked.

The whole class was buzzing after they left. Robin rushed over to Rachel and the two whispered. Kids shouted questions and passed notes, but neither would answer. Ophie started wondering if migraines were something that could kill you. *Ick.* Should she feel sorry for Merry?

Ophie guessed that Rachel must have run to the office after school, because she was nowhere around when Ophie, Tana, and Brittany walked home. Maybe Merry was being wheeled out of the school on an ambulance bed while the red light whirled round and round?

Back in the RV, Brittany made more hats. On her hat, Tana wrote *Dorthy of Oz.* Brittany bent over her hat, stuck out her tongue, and printed *EMT!* Ophie started to write the *D* for *Dorothy,* then changed her mind. She scribbled it out and made the *D* into a lovely red hair ribbon. Then she turned the hat over, wrote *Merry Morshak,* and stuck it on her head.

"I SEE COLORS!" she wailed.

"Should I get help?" asked Tana.

"I can't see! I CAN'T SEE!"

Brittany put a palm on Ophie's forehead. "I think it's a migraine," she said. "We're going to have to get to the hospital quick!"

MERRY tried to stand up, but collapsed on the floor. DOROTHY tugged at her while the EMT took the wheel of the RV.

"Hold on! I'm turning on the siren! *ERRRRRrrrrrrrERRRRRRrrrrrrERRRR!*"

DOROTHY brought out some plastic picnic knives. "The brain surgery isn't working!" she said. MERRY the headache girl was slipping away fast.

"We can't lose her!" yelled the EMT, frantically turning the steering wheel.

"To Ophie Peeler I leave my blue velvet ice-skater outfit with the fake fur!" said MERRY.

"No!" said DOROTHY.

"Yes!" said MERRY. "And she'll have to take my place on TV too . . ." Her eyelids fluttered. "Tell Mommy good-bye," she croaked. Then she screamed a few times, groaned once, and passed out.

"So what do we do now?" said DOROTHY to her sister. "Follow her to heaven?"

"I'm not dead. I'm in a coma!" declared MERRY.

"Shoot. There's nothing I can do with a coma," said the EMT.

It was a pretty good club meeting—a little different than last week. When it turned 5:00, Tana and Brittany hated to take off their hats.

"Maybe we could wear our hats at school," Brittany said.

"Oh, I don't think that would be a good idea," said Ophie.

"Why not? Why can't we wear our hats?" asked Tana.

"Because this club is . . . secret. Ultra-secret, secret, secret," Ophie whispered. "Understand?"

The girls seemed to agree. So the next morning, Ophie was surprised to see Brittany and Tana waiting at the stop sign, wearing paper hats and scowling.

"Hey! Did you guys forget? I told you our club was a secret."

Brittany folded her arms. "But you also said we were still rethinking about the club."

"We decided to wear them *just this once*," Tana said.

"Well, quick, take 'em off!" Ophie said. "Before someone comes."

"Too late," said Tana. "The big girls already made fun of us."

Ophie felt herself wilting as Tana explained how Merry and Rachel had teased them.

Rachel had said it was stupid to wear a hat for a club nobody else would ever want to join.

"And so I told her," said Tana, "that Merry already was a member whether she liked it or not! Because Ophie pretended to be Merry! And that counts!"

"Oh, Tana," said Ophie. "You told her about that?"

"Just that you pretended to be Merry," said Brittany. "And that you made Merry have a headache and croak in the ambulance."

"And then they all got mad and snotty and said how awful it was to make fun of Merry's headache," Tana said. "And how terrible it was to pretend she died. And they were going to tell Miss Fast . . ."

"I NEVER made her DIE!" declared Ophie. "Don't you guys listen? I made her go into a coma! And I wasn't making fun of her! I was acting!"

Tana became very quiet. She hung her head.

"They wouldn't let us explain that part," said Brittany.

Ophie let out a huff. "I don't get you guys. When I talk, who am I talking to? The air? The trees?" She reached over and lifted Brittany's pigtail. "I see there's an EAR here," Ophie said loudly. "But my words don't seem to get *all the way in!*"

"Yowch," said Brittany.

Ophie dropped the braid, feeling suddenly shaky. "I just," she said with a shudder, "I just need to be by myself."

"Can I come too?" asked Brittany.

"No!" said Ophie. "Then I wouldn't be by myself! Geez!" She hurried off.

At school, Ophie was watchful, but Merry never gave her the slightest notice. However, every time Ophie looked up, either Rachel was staring at her with narrowed eyes, or Brittany was just plain staring.

And after recess, when Ophie looked at her corrected vocabulary sentences, she couldn't help but wonder if Miss Fast wasn't a bit *slow*. Every time Ophie handed something in, it came back with picky comments all over the place. Things like: *Is this a* B *or a* P? Could she really think the girl in the sentence is being chased by a ferocious *PEAR?*

At lunch, Brittany tried approaching Ophie. "You still mad?" Brittany asked.

Ophie put on a stony face. "Look here," she said, pointing to her eyes. "Do I look friendly yet?"

"No, you look mad."

"Very good," said Ophie. "See? I shouldn't always have to explain everything to you."

"Then how will I know things?" Brittany asked.

"A real friend would . . . just know," Ophie said. She buried her face in her hands for a long while. When she looked back up, Brittany was gone.

At 3:15, she couldn't pack quickly enough. *Oh, to go home.*

"Ophie," said Miss Fast. "Could I see you for a moment, please?"

Rats. Ophie stood still while all the boys and girls bustled around her.

"Some-one's in tro-uble," singsonged Robin as she passed.

Shut up, Robin Blob-in, thought Ophie as she sat back down and waited for the other kids to leave. Brittany, the last to go out the door, gave her a sad little wave.

When the classroom was empty, Miss Fast walked over and sat sideways in a desk next to Ophie. "Don't worry," she said. "You're not in trouble."

"Oh, good," said Ophie. "Then is it about . . . my vocabulary homework?"

"No, it's not that. I'm just wondering," she said, "if you know just how special Ophelia Peeler is."

Ophie looked over her shoulder for another Ophelia Peeler. "You mean me?" she said, embarrassed.

"Yes, Ophie." Miss Fast smiled. "I'm talking about you."

"Oh." Ophie felt uncomfortable under Miss Fast's gaze, as if she needed more room, or should move back a seat.

Miss Fast smiled again, even more warmly. "Do you know there is just one Ophelia Peeler?"

Ophie quickly nodded.

"And that she doesn't have to be Merry or try so hard? Because she's good enough being Ophie. Just as she is."

"I guess so," said Ophie.

"All you have to be," said Miss Fast, resting her hand on Ophie's arm and giving it a squeeze, "is *yourself*."

Ophie had heard this before, of course. But she wanted to tell Miss Fast what she *didn't* know: that even Principal Dickerson was someone else! She was flaming-haired Rhonda Fleming in her secret heart! "Have you talked to Mrs. Dickerson about this?" asked Ophie gently.

Miss Fast paused a moment. "Oh no, Ophie. This little talk is just between you and me."

"I think maybe you *should* talk to her," urged Ophie.

Ophie watched Miss Fast's smile dissolve. "I'm not sure I understand," she said.

"She can help you!" Ophie explained.

"Help *me*?" said Miss Fast.

"Yeah," said Ophie. She gave Miss Fast her most sympathetic look. "I've talked to her already about being myself, and she helped me. A lot."

Miss Fast was serious now. "Mrs. Dickerson talked to you?"

"Yes! Ask her!" said Ophie. "She's very, very smart. You can ask her right now."

"All right," said Miss Fast, but Ophie could tell she was still pretty confused. She looked down at her watch. "I suppose. Well, maybe it's time for us both to go home."

"Okay!" said Ophie, standing up. "See you tomorrow, Miss Fast!" Relieved, she scurried out of the room.

If only, she wished, they made Mrs. Dickerson in a smaller size . . .

A Lizzy size.

Chapter Eight

Ophie was feeling so alone by Sunday afternoon, she went to the phone twice to call Brittany, but on the third try she remembered that the Borgs had taken their RV to some oceanside village for the weekend. She pressed her nose against the kitchen windowpanes, filling up each square with steam until she could no longer see.

Beepety-beepety-beepety! The phone rang on the wall. Ophie lifted the receiver and said, "Lonely-quiet-boring residence."

"Oh, it can't be that bad, can it, sweetie?"

"Daddy!" Ophie squealed.

"Daughter!" he replied, laughing.

"Will you ever come home?" Ophie asked. She didn't quite know where that question came from.

"Of course I will," said Mr. Peeler. "I've missed you, Ophelia."

Ophie couldn't tell her father that she had partly forgotten to miss him until just right now. "Daddy . . ." she said.

"Yes?"

But Ophie didn't really have anything to say. She just liked saying his name again.

"Is that Daddy?" called Ophie's mom. She rushed into the kitchen with the baby on her hip and gestured for the phone.

"James!" she said. "The baby crawled! Just now! . . . Yes. You know, I think she's quite advanced."

Her mother laughed and jiggled the baby in a little dance.

"No more bronchitis. And she smiles. All the time! I can't believe how much she resembles you in your baby pictures. She's absolutely precious. Oh, you're missing so much."

"Tell him I have a club!" Ophie whispered loudly. "Tell him I learned how to ice-skate!"

Ophie's mother held a finger to her lips. "In a minute," she said.

"Tell him I've GROWN." She held her hand above her head.

Ophie's mom turned her back. "But the baby is starting to sleep through the night! It's quite a relief, actually . . . "

Babies get credit for the dumbest things. Ophie grabbed her mother's sleeve and yanked.

"What, honey?" her mother said a little impatiently.

"Tell Dad how well I'm adjusting."

Her mother raised her eyebrows. "You'll have your turn in a minute, Ophie," she said.

Ophie waited while the conversation apparently turned to Mr. Peeler's job and all the complications he was having setting up new stores. Mrs. Peeler listened and said "Uh-huh" about a million times and "Poor you" and "Oh, Jim!"

Then Ophie's mom stopped jiggling the baby and became very still. "Oh, dear," she said.

"What is it?" asked Ophie.

"This is so disappointing. I know, I know. But another two months?" Mrs. Peeler sank down in a kitchen chair.

Ophie could not believe her ears.

"Mom!" she said. "Let me talk! Let me talk!"

Her mother covered the receiver and gave Ophie a look. "Not now, Ophie. I have to talk to Daddy in private for a moment."

"But the *baby* gets to stay?" said Ophie, stinging.

"Go outside." Her mother pointed sternly to the door.

And with that, Ophie ran out the kitchen door, over the back patio, and into the street until she came to the big, grassy open space called the common. It had benches and a walking path and a little concrete community center. She climbed the steps of the big wooden gazebo, stood dead center, and yelled:

"My parents IGNORE me!"

This felt good.

"I am the LONELIEST girl in the WORLD!" she shouted, her voice bouncing off the wall of the community center.

"I HATE IT HERE!"

" . . . it here . . ."

"I AM NOT ADJUSTING!"

" . . . justing . . ."

"I WISH . . ." Ophie paused as if considering whether to use a nasty word. She took a deep breath.

"I WISH I WAS DEAD!!"

" . . . dead!!"

Ew, shouldn't have said that. The faint echo sounded almost like a voice from the grave.

She looked up at the grumpy gray sky and remembered her last house in Long Beach, before there was a baby. She had Lizzy stay over almost every Saturday. And when her dad called, he spent at least half an hour just talking to her.

Ophie stared into the clouds. "I want my dad back!" she said. "If I can't have Lizzy, then I should get my dad!"

A bit of sunlight streamed through a crack in the mud-colored sky. As Ophie squinted, the beam of light grew. And then, as if the sun shouldered aside the clouds, the light shone down in a golden column. Ophie felt the warmth on her face and watched until she was forced to shut her eyes.

"Boy," she said. She rubbed and blinked. When she was able to focus again, she was gazing down at her shoes. There, right between her shoes, in the crack of the floorboards, Ophie saw something sparkle. She knelt down and stuck her finger in the crack. After a few tries, she finally got hold of the glinting object.

"*Geeeez!*"

The thing was flat and golden. A golden *#1.* Engraved down the center was the word GIRL.

"Number one girl," Ophie said. She looked

up at the sky again. The light had disappeared. "Oh. My. Gosh."

She decided to stand there a few more minutes to see if something else miraculous might happen. And then it started to rain.

Ophie ran, cupping the precious #1 in both hands. Once in a while she'd stop and peek at it, just to make sure she wasn't dreaming. "Boy oh boy oh boy . . ."

Her feet were muddy when she burst through the kitchen door.

"Ophelia, your shoes!" her mother said.

Ophie looked down. She stuffed the #1 into her pocket, took off her shoes, ripped off a paper towel, and began dabbing at her shoe prints.

"Well, thank you, honey," said her mother. "That's so helpful."

Ophie looked at her and smiled. "Does anything else need cleaning?" she asked.

Her mother looked suddenly concerned. "Uh, no, we're fine. But thanks."

Ophie smiled again. "Well, maybe I should go upstairs and make my bed!"

"Oh, sweetie," Ophie's mother said, "please stand up."

Ophie stood and found herself squished in a hug. "I'm sorry," Mrs. Peeler said. "You didn't even get your turn to talk to Daddy."

"That's okay," said Ophie, her voice muffled in her mother's sweater. "When will he be back?"

"Eight more weeks." She hugged Ophie tighter.

And Ophie swore silently that in those eight weeks, she would be the old dependably cheerful Ophie again, but better. If there were noises outside at night, she'd be the one to go look with a flashlight. She'd empty the garbage and the icky diaper pail.

"I'm going to do my homework!" Ophie declared. "Right now."

"Well, all right!" said her mother, beaming.

"See you!" Ophie cried, and ran up the stairs in her stocking feet. The first thing she wanted to do was to get this #1 on a chain to wear around her neck. She had an old silver necklace with a dolphin on it. That would have to do, even though it didn't exactly match.

Ophie slid the gold #1 down the chain, fastened the clasp, and looked in the mirror. She gave the charm a pat, then settled down to do her spelling words, careful to use her most beautiful handwriting.

During homework, Ophie thought about the Borg sisters with a softer heart. She felt herself longing to tell Brittany and Tana about the #1. To Ophie, the event had the makings of a miracle. And who would know more about God and miracles than two girls who went to Sunday school every week?

The next morning, Ophie was the one waiting at the stop sign for the Borgs to show up.

"Hey, Tana! Brittany!" she said.

Brittany cautiously examined Ophie's face. "You don't *look* mad . . ."

"No, I'm not mad," said Ophie. "I forgive you. Do you forgive me?"

"We got to," said Brittany. "It says so in our religion."

"Yes! Religion! Exactly!" Ophie lowered her voice. "Can I tell you guys something?"

"Oh. I can tell this is going to be a good one!" Tana said.

As Ophie launched into her story about the miraculous charm, Brittany and Tana stood speechless.

"So I was thinking," said Ophie, tucking the necklace back into her shirt, "does it say anything in the Bible about things like this? Does God give people presents? Like jewelry?"

"He gave Moses the Ten Commandments," said Tana.

"Did light come out of the clouds?" Ophie asked.

"I think light always comes out of the clouds," said Brittany. "Except if they're night clouds."

"Ooo," said Tana. "This is pretty exciting."

"Maybe I should start going to church?" Ophie suggested.

"*Everybody* should go to church," said Brittany.

Ophie wondered if this could be true. *I'll ask*

the sky about it later. When I'm alone, she thought.

During math, Ophie patted the charm and wondered if she'd make fewer mistakes in long division. Was the miracle going to make her smarter, or give her new talents? Or at recess, for example, could she get to the top floor on Chinese jump rope at last?

Brrr-iiing! First recess. Time to find out!

"Brittany," Ophie said as the kids shuffled out to the playground, "I am going to conduct a test of the charm. And I want you to be a witness."

Brittany stopped dead in her tracks. "Okay," she said, staring intently.

"No, not here," said Ophie. "I want you to watch me at Chinese jump rope. You know how I never get to the sixth floor?"

"Or the fifth floor," Brittany said. "You're not very good."

"I know, I know. But maybe I will be now." She patted her throat where the #1 charm was hidden. "Do you know what I mean?"

"No," said Brittany.

"Maybe things have changed . . . since the *miracle*." Ophie gave Brittany a conspiratorial nudge.

"Well, you better get in line right now," said Brittany. "It's gonna be a long wait."

Ophie was one of the last girls to get a place. First in line, of course, was Merry.

"One, two, three, four! In, click, out—KILL!" chanted the girls. Merry did a perfect kill, pinning the jump rope with the soles of her feet until it rolled all the way down to the asphalt. Now for the sixth floor.

The jump rope, a long circle of elastic, was hiked up around the girls' hips. Merry squinted, and leaped up with a "Yah!" but only jumped high enough to hit the rope with her knees.

"Oh, pooh," Merry muttered.

Ha! thought Ophie.

"Two and a half minutes until the bell," said Brittany when Ophie's turn came. Ophie tried breathing out really hard to get rid of her nervousness. Then she glanced up at the sky and said, "It's all up to you."

First floor was a cinch. As soon as she took the first leap, she felt a remarkable sense of calm. Second floor was just as easy. Third and fourth seemed to require much less effort than usual. *I'm bouncing like a Super Ball,* thought Ophie. *And I'm not even really trying.*

Fifth floor? Just a three-foot leap in the air. *I'm under a spell,* she thought. *A miracle jumping spell.*

"One, two, three, four! In, click, out, KILL!"

Fifth floor—done! Ophie wanted to look over at Brittany, but thought it might jinx her.

"One, two, three, four!"

Ophie paused. The rope was now as high as her hips. She clenched her fists and jumped.

"IN!" shouted the girls.

Ophie gave a scissors kick.

"CLICK!" they yelled.

She leaped and straddled the ropes.

"OUT!"

Ophie squeezed her eyes shut, opened them, and gave a tremendous "YAH!"

"KILL!" shouted the crowd.

Ophie could see the rope beneath her shoes, sliding down floor by floor. *Yes, yes, yes!* She hit the ground—*STOMP!*—feeling victorious. "WHOO-HOO!" She raised her fist in the air and looked around, expecting to bask in victory. But the faces on all the girls had gone blank. Ophie looked down quickly. Her left toe had slipped off the rope. She was short of a kill by two inches.

"No," she said. "No!" She bent over and touched the rope in disbelief. She stood up quickly, and found herself face-to-face with Merry Morshak, who stood glaring at her, one hand over her mouth.

"My . . . charm!" Merry gasped. "Rachel, look . . . Ophie Peeler stole my charm!"

Ophie clasped her throat. "I did not!"

"You did so . . . you STEALER," said Merry. "Look, it doesn't even match her chain!"

"How could you?" asked Rachel. "That charm is fourteen-karat gold!"

"My mother had that made for me. For my birthday. I didn't have it for more than a week," said Merry.

"I'M NOT A STEALER!" hollered Ophie. Even her fingertips felt fiery hot.

"I'll bet," said Robin, horning her way in, "the charm fell off when Ophie was following you two home from school and she just snatched it up. That's what I think."

"That's a lie!" said Ophie. "I don't follow you home! Maybe you guys follow ME home!" Unfortunately, she realized at once how ridiculous that sounded.

Rachel rolled her eyes. Merry just stood there looking mad and a little scary.

"I found it at the gazebo. On Sunday," said Ophie softly.

"Merry and Rachel play at the gazebo!" squealed Robin. "Isn't that right, Merry?"

Merry stretched out her hand. "Just give it back," she said.

The recess bell rang, but the crowd of girls didn't budge. Ophie looked around at all the blaming faces and couldn't move either. Then Brittany came up from behind. Ophie felt Brittany's hands undo the clasp at the back of her neck. Then she watched as Brittany stepped over to Merry and put the necklace in her hand.

"I don't need the chain," said Merry, holding it between her thumb and finger like something stinky.

"I'll take it," said Brittany. "It belongs to Ophie."

Brittany fastened the naked chain back on Ophie's neck.

"Thank you," Ophie said in a shaky voice.

The TV Girls left, taking the entire crowd of fourth-grade girls with them.

Ophie cleared her throat and tried a smile. "I guess that wasn't a miracle after all."

"Yes, it was," declared Brittany, sturdy and serious, standing with her hands on her hips. "I've seen you play Chinese jump rope. It's a miracle you got to the *fifth* floor."

"Well, maybe," said Ophie. "Thanks." It was a nice thing to say. A friend-type thing.

Chapter Nine

Today, Miss Fast was giving everyone in class a chance to "Show-and-tell—with a twist." She called this assignment: "I'm the Kind of Person Who . . ."

Ophie watched as Miss Fast stood in front of the class and gave her own report.

"Hello, I'm Miss Fast. I'm the kind of person who . . . loves mystery novels." She held up a book.

Ophie couldn't believe it. *Miss Fast is a fan of* D is for DEATH?

"I take a mystery novel with me everywhere. I read mystery novels while I wait at the doctor's office. I read mystery novels when I'm in line at the bank. To me, time is never wasted if I can spend it with a mystery novel!"

Hmmm, thought Ophie. *What am I going to say?*

"What kind of person are you?" Ophie asked Brittany.

"Tall," said Brittany. "What kind of person are you?"

"I'm still deciding," said Ophie.

"I'd say you're medium-size," said Brittany.

"Uh, thanks, Brittany."

Could she really do a show-and-tell about being average height?

All week Ophie thought about what kind of person she could say she was. She liked bubble baths—but she couldn't get up in front of a class and talk about *naked* stuff.

By the time she walked home on Wednesday, she thought, *I am the kind of person who is . . . running out of time.* Traipsing up her driveway with her head down, she bumped right into a UPS man.

"Ooof!" said Ophie. "Sorry. I wasn't looking."

"That's okay, short stuff. You live here?" asked the man. He had a package under his arm.

Ophie checked out his badge, his brown shorts, and his official UPS truck before answering. "Yes," she said.

"The sign says I'm not supposed to ring the bell. Do you think you could go in and get Ophelia Peeler to sign for this?"

"I'm Ophelia Peeler!" said Ophie.

"Great!" The man handed her a pen. Ophie signed and took the package. It had tiny Japanese characters in vertical rows on one of its labels. And in the corner, there was a big logo for Mercury Athletic Shoes.

"This must be from my dad," Ophie said.

"Well, it's all yours now," the man said. He gave her a wink.

Ophie walked in to find her mother asleep on the couch. She tiptoed to the kitchen with the package. She thrust her hand deep into the box until she felt a long, hard roll of paper, shiny and thickish, like a magazine cover. Ophie slid the rubber band off and unrolled it.

It was a poster—a poster of three teenage American boys. Ophie couldn't read the Japanese characters written down the side of the picture, but she did notice that each of the boys had signed an autograph.

Konichiwa, Ophie! Love, Ryan

Ophie Peeler rocks! xxx, Jordan

Love to our favorite American fan!! ☺ Kyle

Ophie plunged her hand into the box again and fished around for something else. She felt the corners of another box! "Oh good!" she cried, scattering Styrofoam pellets everywhere.

THE BAILEY BROZ DAY CALENDAR! Spend a day, every day, with JORDAN! RYAN! and KYLE! 365 HUNK-DeeLISHUS Days a Year!

"It's just those guys again!" sighed Ophie. She flipped through the pages.

October 3rd—*Ryan and Jordy like Jamoca*

Almond Fudge; but Kyle sez, Gimme banana anything!

July 2nd—LUV FAX—Kyle likes short girls! Ryan likes athletic types. And Jordan has NEVER dated a blonde!

"Daddy sent me this?" said Ophie. She flipped to the date of her birthday:

August 7th—"Your day, OPHIE!" "Ophie, you ROCK!" "Happy birthday, SWEET Ophie!"

Kyle, Jordan, and Ryan had written all over the page.

"I rock?" repeated Ophie. "I *rock . . .*"

Did Dad make these Bailey Broz do this? Could I get up in front of class tomorrow and say, "Hello, I'm Ophie Peeler. I'm the kind of person who . . . ROCKS"?

"Ophie, what've you got there?" Ophie's mom stood in the doorway.

"I don't really know. Who are the Bailey . . . Brahz?"

Ophie's mom took the poster and squinted. "Oh, I think you pronounce that Bailey *BROZE*—you know, like bro, brother."

"These guys are brothers?"

"They must be some kids promoting shoes for Daddy's company over in Japan. They're probably in a band." Mrs. Peeler picked up the Bailey Broz Daily Calendar and peeled off a sticky note from the bottom.

"Ophie," she read, "I thought you might know who these guys were. They filmed a commercial at our store in Tokyo. See you soon, love Daddy."

"Well then, I guess I'm the kind of person who . . . likes to get packages?" Would that work?

* * *

Ophie noticed that she wasn't the only one carrying something to school the next morning. A small boy named Wesley dragged in a heavy black case with something called a fluegelhorn inside. A big group of boys surrounded him, begging him to let them blow into it.

The girls were much more excited about Merry's bundle. She was carrying a shiny red carry-all that had a just-new-from-the-store look. *International Girl* was stamped on the side in silver. Even Miss Fast seemed excited about Merry's bundle. She *did* call on her first . . .

"Hello, my name is Merry Morshak." She paused and grinned as if she were posing for a school picture. "I'm the kind of person who . . . collects everything for my Ingrid doll from International Girl. I'm too old to play with dolls, but I am keeping this to give to my children. Because Ingrid is a collectible doll."

Ophie looked around. Almost all the girls sat expectantly at the edges of their seats. Except, of course, Brittany, who sat, as usual, like someone waiting for a bus.

"This is Ingrid's carrying case. It is also"— here Merry undid the latches—"Ingrid's bedroom."

The girls "ooohed" when the case unfolded. The walls were papered in a pink print, which matched the tiny furniture. Merry took her genuine Ingrid doll, dressed in flannel pajamas and a pink woolen bed jacket, and sat her on the mattress.

"She has everything she needs for a morning of eating breakfast in bed." Merry held up a tiny plate. "This is her lutefisk."

"Blech," said Brittany decisively.

Merry, looking peeved, turned to Miss Fast.

"Did you have something to say, Brittany?" asked Miss Fast.

"Lutefisk," said Brittany. "They made me eat it at Christmas once. But not anymore."

"Why is that?"

"Because I threw up," said Brittany.

Ophie noticed this made everyone laugh—except Merry.

"Lutefisk," said Miss Fast in a voice loud enough to carry over the chuckling, "is a Swedish treat."

" . . . that makes you throw up," Brittany insisted. She crossed her arms.

"INGRID does NOT throw up! She is a DOLL," said Merry.

The kids laughed again. Merry snapped the

case closed and returned to her seat with a flounce and none of her usual smile.

"Class, if there are questions or comments you have for 'I'm the Kind of Person Who . . .' please hold them until after the presentation is over." Miss Fast gave Merry a sympathetic glance. "Now, Ophie, what would you like to share?"

I'm the kind of person, thought Ophie, *who . . . just wants to get this thing over with.* She picked up her UPS box and clumped to the front of the class.

"I'm Ophelia Peeler," she said dully, "and I'm the kind of person who . . . receives packages in the mail." She opened the box and pulled out the poster. "My dad sent me this," she said, unrolling the coil of paper. "It has Japanese writing on it."

"AAAAAaaaiiiiEEEEEEEEeeeeeeee!!!!"

A piercing squeal. Ophie flinched. She let the poster roll up like a window shade.

"Was that . . . the Bailey Broz?" asked Rachel Peacock, her voice quavering.

Ophie couldn't believe the look on her face. "Uh, yes, it is." She unrolled the poster again. "See? It's them. They wrote stuff on it."

"Aaaaagh! What does it say?" squeaked Robin.

"Please, girls," interrupted Miss Fast.

"It says," Ophie read, pointing to Jordan, *"Ophie Peeler rocks."*

Ophie watched, amazed, as Merry's jaw dropped. The TV Girls were gawking *at her*.

"And they also gave me a calendar," said Ophie, beginning to relish the moment. "And they wrote all over it on my birthday day. And, um, they said I was their favorite American fan."

Merry and Rachel looked at each other as if they'd been simultaneously socked in the stomach. Robin actually seemed to be turning pale.

Ophie quickly rolled up the poster and put it back in the box. "That's all!" she said briskly. She pressed her lips tightly together and smiled, hoping to look cool enough.

Laura, the girl who had not said boo to

Ophie since the skating party, gave her an admiring smile. "Wow," she said.

"How do you know those boys?" Brittany asked.

"I *don't*," said Ophie.

"They sound like they know you," said Brittany.

"I know. But it's really just, you know, *advertising*."

Ophie was surprised to be very popular on the playground that day. Girls like Robin who already knew the Bailey Broz were having fits of envy. And the girls who didn't know anything about them yet wanted to get in on the excitement. It turns out that these boys had a song on the radio. And the name of the song was "She Rocks!"

"Oh, come on!" Robin said to Brittany. "You've never heard it before?"

"I have," said a small voice. It was Charlotte Camp, peeking shyly through her red bangs.

The TV Girls had been keeping their distance, standing just close enough to the mob surrounding Ophie to eavesdrop. But Rachel could stand it no more.

"Even *Charlotte* knows!" said Rachel

"Okay, Rachel," said Ophie coolly. "Do you know how it goes?"

"Of course," Rachel said.

"Well, sing it, then!" said Ophie.

Rachel was blushing—actually blushing.

"Really! Sing it!" said Ophie. "Show us!"

The crowd closed in around Rachel. "Sing!" they cried.

"She rocks!" Rachel croaked tentatively.

The crowd whooped.

"She so rocks! She's a hottie, she's a super-fox!" Rachel sort of crooned. Some of the kids began to clap in time.

"She's sweet! Something-something . . . off my feet . . ."

The crowd continued to clap, waiting for the rest. Rachel shifted from foot to foot. "That's all I know," she said.

"*Awwwwwww* . . ." said the crowd.

"There's a lot more words than that! Right,

Ophie?" Laura said, looking to Ophie as if she were some old friend.

Rachel, shamefaced, went back to stand with Merry.

"They play it on KISS-FM all the time," Charlotte added, this time with actual confidence.

Ophie made a mental note of that. At the end of the day, she carried the box on her shoulder and whistled half the way home.

"You sure are whistling a lot," said Brittany.

"I'm happy!" said Ophie.

"But you never whistled before," said Brittany.

"Well, I haven't been whistling happy."

"What's that?" asked Brittany.

"It's a better kind of happy," said Ophie, feeling exasperated. "You know, like birthday happy or getting a new cat happy or . . ."

"When they run out of lutefisk before it gets to you happy," added Brittany, catching on.

"Yes, Brittany, that's *it* exactly!" said Ophie. You know, sometimes—"

"Hey, Ophie!" someone called.

Ophie looked over her shoulder. Across the street were Rachel and the one-and-only Merry. But this time, they were smiling. At her!

"What?" said Ophie. She looked down to see if she had tucked her sweater in her underpants or if her shoes were untied. "I mean, hi!" she said.

"Want to walk home with us?" said Rachel Peacock. She gave a little nod as if to say, *Of course you would, wouldn't you?*

Ophie pointed to her chest. "Me?"

"Yes," said Merry. "Just you."

Ophie stopped abruptly and crossed her arms. "First, tell me how come," she demanded. *No one* walked home with Rachel and Merry. Not even Robin.

"Because . . ." said Merry, popping her flashbulb grin, "we want to talk to you about your singing, and maybe you want to be on TV?"

"Really?" Ophie reached over and squeezed Brittany's arm. "Can you believe this?" she whispered.

Ophie felt a grin take over her face and her heart thump as she stepped off the curb. She hesitated a moment, then kept going.

She didn't look back.

Chapter Ten

Mmmmph, morning already?

Ophie had spent last night with the radio under her pillow, listening to KISS-FM, waiting for the Bailey Broz. Their song didn't play until 11:55 P.M. Ophie wanted to memorize the words in case the TV Girls brought it up.

"Rock! I so rock!" Ophie combed her hair and sang to herself in the mirror. Merry and Rachel had invited her to meet them at the gazebo that morning in order to take their "secret" shortcut to school. She packed her Bailey Broz day calendar with the writing all over it, ate her breakfast so quickly she couldn't taste it—and ran!

No one was there. She checked her wristwatch. She was probably a little too early. Ophie sat and tapped her foot, humming, thinking of how she could bring up maybe making the Cadillac commercial duet into a trio.

She was starting to wonder if the girls had ditched her, when she spotted Merry's red jacket. Ophie leaped up and hopped and waved. "Hi!" she shouted. "Hi! I'm here!"

Upon sighting Ophie, the TV Girls appeared to slow down.

"Over here!" Ophie cried. "Hey, you guys!"

The girls dawdled over.

"Thought you didn't see me," said Ophie, panting.

"Oh, we saw you, Ophie," said Rachel.

"So, how long have you been standing here?" asked Merry.

"Uh, I've been here about ten minutes," she said. "Just thinking, having ideas."

"Well, you don't have to be so early," said Rachel.

"Let's go," said Merry.

But there wasn't room on the sidewalk for all three of them. Ophie found herself picking her way over lawns and up against hedges.

"Did you bring your calendar?" Merry asked.

"Yeah!" said Ophie, ducking a tree branch. "Got it right here in my backpack. Hey, did anyone else listen to KISS-FM last night at eleven fifty-five?"

"I go to sleep at nine p.m.," said Merry. "Always."

"Oh," said Ophie. "The Bailey Broz were on. I mean, OUR Bailey Broz were on." She waited in case there was a reaction. "And I started thinking: Isn't it great that there are three Bailey Broz and three of us? And then I thought, hey! Isn't that funny how we're ALL singers too? Anyway—"

"Merry," interrupted Rachel, "my mom wants to know if your mom signed you up for horse camp yet."

"I signed up a couple weeks ago," said Merry.

"Oh, good. Anyway, my mom made them promise that they'd save Windy for me," said Rachel, "because my horse last year was so bad."

"You reserved *Windy*?" said Merry.

Rachel seemed to freeze. "Well, yes. I mean, my mom did."

"Where does it say on the form that you can *reserve* horses?"

"I don't know. I didn't read the form," said Rachel.

"If you can reserve horses," said Merry, "my mother would have reserved one. And she would have reserved Windy! Because I've always gotten Windy. I cannot *believe* that you—"

"So you guys like horses?" asked Ophie.

The girls gave her a killing look.

"I'm just wondering," said Ophie, faltering, "because I think they are kinda scary."

The girls remained silent.

"They've got those giant teeth!" Ophie babbled. "You know, *chomp, ouch!* Kinda scary and—"

"Merry," said Rachel pointedly, "maybe your mom can reserve you another horse. What about Thunder?"

"I don't want Thunder," said Merry.

As the back-and-forth about Windy and Thunder continued all the way to school, Ophie studied Rachel and Merry, the way they walked with their arms folded. Ophie folded her arms too, and then waited, determined to bring up the Cadillac commercials again at the first opportunity.

There was something so satisfying about casually walking down the halls with Merry and Rachel. But while the TV Girls walked with their chins up, ignoring the fact that everyone looked to see them pass, Ophie basked in the attention.

"Ha, ha, ha!" Ophie chuckled in a stagy sort of way to show everyone how much she was enjoying herself.

"What's so funny?" asked Rachel.

"Oh, nothing! Just that thing you said about . . . the homework!" Ophie flashed a Merry-type smile. "Boy! I hate it too!"

"Most people do," said Merry dryly.

"Oooh, but I *really* hate it." Ophie made a goofy face and gave herself a clownish bop on the head.

Once she reached the classroom, however, Ophie felt a rush of guilt. "Hey, Brittany," she said, giving an awkward wave.

Brittany was already seated. "I was at the stop sign this morning," she said.

"Uh, you were?" said Ophie.

"Where were you?"

"Who wants to know?" Ophie blustered.

Brittany looked bewildered. *"Me,"* she said. "And Tana."

"I don't have to walk to school the same way every day."

"True," said Brittany in a voice so mild, it made Ophie feel terrible.

At lunch, Ophie sat with the TV Girls. She placed her calendar in the middle of the table and they passed it around, discussing who was the cutest-ever Bailey Bro.

"I like Jordan," said Merry. "Because blue eyes look really good with black hair."

"I like Kyle," said Rachel. "Because he's the best singer."

"Well, he's not as cute as Jordan," said Merry. "But it's only fair. After all, you DID get Windy . . ."

"Then I guess I'll like Ryan," said Ophie.

She sipped her milk as the two girls wrangled about horses. Ophie began crossing her eyes. With two of everyone, the arguing seemed a little more dramatic.

"Ophie! What are you doing?" demanded Merry.

Ophie let the two pinched Merry faces dissolve back into one. "Crossing my eyes," she said.

"Well, stop it," Merry said. "It's weird."

Ophie glanced over at Brittany, holding open her bag of chips so Tana could share. *That's the sort of thing Lizzy and I would do.* What would happen if she just reached over into Merry's bag of chips? *Eek. Better not.*

On the way home, the TV Girls were still all about horse camp, making it impossible for Ophie to break in.

"You guys . . ." Ophie began, but the girls went on talking. So Ophie cleared her throat. And then she started coughing. Hacking, really.

"What is up with you?" said Rachel.

"'Scuse me," said Ophie. "I have to go now."

"Okay," said Rachel.

"Wait," Ophie said. "Hey, do you want a surprise?"

"What kind of surprise?" asked Merry.

Ophie started nervously snapping her fingers. "Uhhh," she said. " . . . a Bailey Broz surprise?"

"Do you have more stuff?" Merry said.

"Oh, I have better than that!" said Ophie. "Way better. Just come over to my house on Saturday and I'll show you."

"I'm always at the rink on Saturday. Lessons," said Merry.

"Well, after the rink, then," said Ophie. "Come over for this wonderful, fantastic . . . thing!"

Merry paused, then agreed to show up at four o'clock. Then Rachel said she would too.

"It'll be great!" Ophie shouted after them. Not until they were out of sight did Ophie whisper under her breath, "I *think* . . ."

That evening, Ophie ran to her parents' bedroom and jerked open her father's bureau drawer. "What would Jordan wear?" she murmured. If only she could find something with a Mercury Athletic Logo. Nothing. She held up an old T-shirt that said *Terry's Tile and Concrete.* Maybe she could say a Bailey Bro took off this T-shirt and left it behind? *Nah.*

"Aye, yi yi." Ophie pulled out a goofy pair of argyle socks, a golf tee, a tiny tin of extra-strength Excedrin, a pair of mittens . . .

Mittens! Those were the kind of things people were always leaving behind. Ophie could never see her dad ever wearing these. She wondered why he even had them. They were bulky with a leather patch on the palm.

She took one mitten, stuffed it under her shirt, and tiptoed back to her bedroom. *Now I really am a stealer.* Ophie allowed herself that thought for a moment, then hid the glove in a bottom drawer and tried to forget about it.

For the next few days, Ophie got by by being quiet and keeping her arms folded. And it was sort of nice being in on the TV Girls' little privileges—like when Robin gave her cuts in the lunch line. But she didn't ask to sing on TV. She knew she wasn't "in" enough for that—yet.

* * *

On Saturday morning Ophie spent extra time making her bedroom look its best. After setting her ruby slippers on a footstool in the corner, she hung the Bailey Broz poster over her bed. The Official Bailey Broz Daily Calendar was displayed on her desk with a study lamp spotlighting it. The one thing she didn't have, but wished she did, were trophies. Trophies would have been great. Or ribbons.

Didn't horse girls always have lots of those hanging around their bedrooms?

Ophie grabbed a pair of scissors and opened her closet door. Hanging there was a black party dress she wore the Christmas before last. A red ribbon sash hung from the waist. She chopped the ribbon into two strips. With a felt pen she wrote the words *FIRST PLACE*.

The first ribbon didn't turn out too well. Her lettering was too big and got squished-looking near the letter *E*. The next ribbon was better. Ophie hung both of them on the blank spaces of her bulletin board. She dusted off her hands and looked around the room. It looked good!

At a little after four o'clock, Merry and Rachel were at the front door. Ophie peeked at them through the spy hole. They rang twice.

"Aren't you going to answer the door?" Ophie's mother called.

Ophie practiced a happy face. She flung open the door. "You're here!" she cried.

Rachel and Merry walked into the entryway.

"So, what's the surprise?" asked Merry.

"In my room," said Ophie. "Follow me."

The girls walked together in a clump, always a few feet behind Ophie. Then they stood just outside her bedroom door.

"C'mon!" said Ophie.

Once inside, however, the girls had their hands all over everything.

"Gee, do you think it's pink enough in here?" Merry said, poking the wall and shading her eyes.

"And why is this Barbie wearing a green sock?" asked Rachel, dangling Ophie's doll by the hair.

"My best friend did that for me when we were in third grade," Ophie said. "She's the Little Mermaid. See?" She took back the doll and smoothed her tresses. "It isn't a sock. It's her tail."

"And what is this?" Merry had taken down the First Place ribbon and turned it over in her hand.

"Oh. It's from my old school," Ophie said casually.

"First place in what?" asked Merry.

"First place in singing," Ophie said, without missing a beat. "The talent show." She pointed to the other ribbon. "And this is for best actress. But no *commercials,* like you guys . . . yet."

Merry dropped the ribbon on the desk. "Hey, what are those?" She sauntered over to the corner and picked up one ruby slipper.

"I think . . . you'd better put that down," Ophie said quickly.

"Why?" asked Merry.

"They're very special old antique collectible expensive . . . collectibles."

"You already said that," said Rachel.

"Yes, I know. But they *are* very valuable and"—Ophie wrenched the shoe from Merry's hand—"NOT for touching!"

"Okay! I get it," said Merry, holding up her hands.

"So, Ophie," said Rachel. "Where is the surprise?"

"Yeah," said Merry. "*Is* there a surprise?"

"Yes, there is," Ophie said, composing herself. "I have something very special," she continued, "from someone very special. He is a friend of mine and a friend of my family. He likes ice cream and snowboarding, and he has never dated a blonde. And he's cute too."

"Jordan!" said Merry.

Ophie tucked her red shoe under her arm, opened her desk drawer, and pulled out the mitten. "So now we know something else about Jordan," she said, holding the prize above her head.

"What, he skis?" guessed Merry.

Ophie gazed at the big, overstuffed glove. "Well, sometimes. Maybe," she said. "But what I was going to tell you is that he gets really cold hands. And that he is forgetful. And one more thing!" said Ophie, hoping she had built enough suspense. "THIS IS JORDAN'S MITTEN!"

"No!" said Merry as Rachel gasped.

"And Jordan left this at my dad's store. And my dad sent it to me for a souvenir. And just THINK! Jordan, the cutest Bailey Bro, had his hand in here! There are probably still germs in here that belong to JORDAN!"

"Can I see that?" asked Merry, reaching.

"Better than that!" said Ophie. "YOU CAN HAVE IT!"

"*Aaaiiiiiieeeeee!*" Merry and Rachel screamed. Then Merry took the glove and slid it over her fingers. It was a humongous mitten, especially capping the end of Merry's skinny arm.

"I thought it was silly of me to keep it, since YOU have dibs on Jordan."

"Look!" said Rachel. "It has a little clip on it!"

"I can hang it from my backpack!" said Merry.

"And maybe I can get other stuff from Kyle and Ryan," said Ophie. "You know, all I have to do is ask my dad."

"I would take anything from Kyle!" declared Rachel.

"Could you get mine signed?" Merry asked.

"Okay, okay. I'll see what Dad can do."

Merry stood up, still admiring the clunky

mitten. "Well, this was a pretty good surprise after all." With that, she walked out of Ophie's bedroom and down the stairs. Rachel scurried behind.

Merry got to the entryway and paused. "Ophie, you know what would be cool?"

"What?" said Ophie.

"You know how my dad does advertising? For his cars?"

Ophie nodded, feeling the heat rising to her cheeks.

"So do you think that maybe your dad could get the Bailey Broz to appear with you and me and Rachel in OUR commercial?"

Merry and Rachel began jumping up and down.

Ophie winced. "Gee, I really don't know. They're pretty busy. Don't you think we could just make a commercial with the three of us?"

"Oh, please, please!" begged Merry.

"All right, then. I'll try," Ophie lied.

"You get the Bailey Broz, Peeler, and you'll be in our commercial *for sure*." said Merry.

"What do you mean, for sure?" Ophie asked.

"Just what I said. See you at school on Monday," called Merry.

"At the gazebo, Ophie," said Rachel. "But not too early."

Ophie stood in the doorway and watched the girls as they took turns touching the glove. They giggled and talked in low voices between themselves.

Ophie sighed. More time with the TV Girls. More possible chances at commercials.

That was good.

Right?

Ophie looked down and realized that she still had the ruby slipper in her hand. The shoes were almost as perfect and pretty as the day she first wore them onstage.

She slowly closed the front door, sat on the entryway bench, and pulled off her tennis shoe and sock. Daintily pointing her toe, Ophie wiggled into the ruby slipper. *Ow.* She stood up and tried again. Her heel crushed down the back of the shoe. Finally, Ophie sat down and shoved on the shoe with her hand until she had to give up.

I can't believe it, she thought. *They don't fit.*

She stared at the slipper, then lifted it to her face. The silk was cool and smooth against her cheek. *They're not really mine anymore. Just another memory,* she thought. She spent the rest of the day un-arranging her room and feeling, somehow, a bit lost.

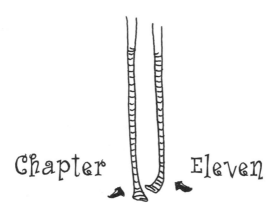

Chapter Eleven

Walking to school with the TV Girls gave Ophie a lot of time to think because she wasn't doing any talking or listening. The arguments and stories of horse camp and ice-skating had all become one big blur.

This day, Ophie spent the walk memorizing how to dodge all the branches and bushes she was crammed up against. She kept her arms wrapped around herself tightly. *It's hard, keeping this quiet.*

She watched Jordan's giant mitten swishing back and forth, back and forth, from Merry's backpack. *I am getting sleeeeeeepy. . . . My eye-lids are getting heavy. . . .*

"Ophie!"

"Huh?" said Ophie.

Rachel cocked her head. *"Hello!"* she said. "You heard from your dad yet?"

"Yes," said Ophie. "Why?"

"Why?" Rachel laughed. "Why do you think?"

"Um, I'm working on it," Ophie said.

"Well, can you work faster?" asked Rachel.

"Oh, brother," said Merry as they neared the school. "Why is Brittany Borg always staring at us? Ophie, can't you get her to stop?"

"Me?" said Ophie. "I can't stop her."

"Oh, yes you could," said Rachel, "if you wanted to."

"No, really," said Ophie. "You don't know her."

"Yeah, and I never will," Rachel said.

"You know," said Merry, "I think you still like Brittany."

"You do?" said Ophie.

"Well, how hard can it be to go over there

164

and say, 'Stop staring at me and my friends'?"

"It wouldn't be hard, exactly . . ." said Ophie, reddening.

"Hmmm," said Rachel. "But I still don't see you going over there and telling her."

"Honestly!" Merry said. "It's getting creepy. You go over there and let her know. We'll wait."

"Oh, ALL RIGHT!" said Ophie. "Just watch me!" She balled up her fists and marched over to Brittany.

"Peeler?" said Brittany. She had a bright, expectant look on her face that Ophie had not anticipated.

"Brittany," Ophie said. "I have to ask you . . . ask you something."

"Okay!" said Brittany.

Ophie squeezed her eyes shut. "Please stop staring at me and my friends."

Ophie opened her eyes. The bright look on Brittany's face was gone.

"Say that again," Brittany said.

"My friends," said Ophie, feeling sickened,

"they, uh, want me to tell you to stop staring at us."

Brittany nodded. "Okay, then," she said, and turned away. Tana, who was standing nearby, rushed to her sister's side.

Ophie stood frozen. *That's that*, she said to herself. *That's that.* She went back to the TV Girls, but didn't meet their eyes.

"Well, you did it!" said Rachel.

"That's a relief," said Merry. "C'mon."

But Ophie didn't feel relieved, and when Merry actually tugged at Ophie's sleeve and spoke to her—in front of everybody—Ophie knew that this was her *Morshak moment*, a kind of reward. And then Robin sneaked up behind.

"I guess you believe in cooties after all, Peeler," she said. She gave her a snotty-Robin smile.

It was all Ophie could do not to stomp on her stupid snotty foot.

★ ★ ★

"This morning," said Miss Fast as the boys

166

and girls took their seats, "I have a special announcement. Please listen carefully. I'd hate for anyone to be left out . . ."

At this, Ophie tried to peek over at Brittany but couldn't quite see her.

"I have here the permission slips for our big field trip." Miss Fast waved the sheaf of papers. "We are going to visit the new Pioneer Museum and Interpretive Center next Monday! We will leave at eight-thirty a.m."

"Yay!" said Tyler.

"And you are to bring a lunch, because we will be gone all day," continued Miss Fast.

"HOORAAAAAAYYYY!!!" The class went wild.

"Indoor voices, please," said Miss Fast, waiting for the hubbub to die down. "Now, you will have to bring this form back signed, or you may not attend. So please, don't delay. Bring the forms in as soon as possible."

I'm usually the kind of person who loves field trips, thought Ophie. But this news just left her feeling blah.

The blah wouldn't go away. Not after a night's sleep. Not after eating twelve Fig Newtons. Not even when Ophie's dad called.

"It won't be long now," said Ophie's father. "I'll be home and you'll have a regular father to go along with your regular school and your permanent address. Isn't that great?"

"Yeah, great," said Ophie.

"You don't sound so sure," he said. "Don't tell me you've grown accustomed to life on your own already. I AM coming home, you know, honey. I hope you'll still recognize me."

"Yes, I'll recognize you," Ophie said. *But will you recognize the new blah me?*

The next day as Ophie was slowly shuffling back from P.E., Mrs. Dickerson stopped her in the hall to ask her what was wrong.

"Ophelia!" she said.

As soon as Ophie heard Mrs. Dickerson's voice, she tried to rearrange her expression.

"Where's the joie de vivre?" Mrs. Dickerson asked.

"What's the jaw DV?" asked Ophie.

"It's French for *love of life*," she said.

"Oh," said Ophie. "Um, where is it? I . . . don't know."

She gave Ophie a pat on the shoulder. "Well, dear, we all have our bad days."

"I know I do," Ophie said.

Ophie wondered if Mrs. Dickerson was still partly Rhonda Fleming. Because Ophie knew she was less Dorothy than ever.

Mrs. Dickerson started to walk away. Ophie blurted, "They don't fit anymore!"

Mrs. Dickerson turned around. "What doesn't fit?"

Ophie drew closer and whispered, "The red shoes. I tried them on the other day and my feet are too big."

"Ah. The Dorothy shoes, right?" said Mrs. Dickerson in a new, confidential tone.

"Uh-huh. And I put them in the closet so I won't look at them anymore. Because they make me too sad," said Ophie.

"Hmmm . . . really? Because I'm wondering if there might be another way to feel about them." Mrs. Dickerson tapped her forehead. "Now, as I remember, Dorothy didn't need the ruby slippers at the end. And it was a happy ending, wasn't it?"

"Yes," Ophie agreed. "The shoes got her back to her real home, Kansas . . ."

"And those definitely weren't Kansas sort of shoes, were they?" said Mrs. Dickerson.

"Nope," said Ophie, wishing this conversation were making her feel better. She looked around. The rest of the girls were already back in class. "Oops! I'm late!" she said.

"Don't worry. You can tell Miss Fast you have Mrs. Dickerson's permission!"

"Thank you!" said Ophie. "Bye!"

★ ★ ★

At home, Ophie holed up in her room until dinner. When her mother called to her, she pretended not to hear.

"Ophie!" her mother called again. "Could you come down, please? To the dining room!"

Weird. They had *never* eaten in the dining room before. Curious, she padded down the stairs and was startled to see the dining room table set with . . . pink napkins and candles? And Ophie recognized the wonderful smell coming from the kitchen.

"Surprise!" her mother said. She was holding a casserole with two heavy oven mitts. "Cannelloni!"

"Is Daddy coming?" Ophie asked.

"No, not yet," said Mrs. Peeler. She set down the hot dish on a folded kitchen towel. "I just thought this might be a fun way to break in the dining room. It's a two-girl dinner."

"What about Callie?"

"She's asleep for now," said her mother.

"So this is for me?"

"Yes. Just for you."

Ophie looked at her mother, so unexpectedly pretty with her pearly earrings and her orange fuzzy sweater. "You dressed up for *me*?"

Mrs. Peeler walked over, sat down, and took Ophie's hand. "I hoped I could make you happy," she said. "Because I've noticed that lately—you're *not*."

"Well," Ophie said, smiling tightly, "you noticed right."

"I have something for you, Ophie." Mrs. Peeler reached into her pocket and pulled out a sunshine-yellow envelope.

Without warning, Ophie felt hot tears well up. One dribbled from her right eye. "Lizzy," she said, quickly wiping her cheek with the back of her hand.

"Here," her mother said. "It's yours."

Ophie took the envelope in her hand and turned it over. Lizzy had drawn a rainbow in colored pencil on the back. A bluebird held a sign in its beak. *Come back, Ophie Peeler!* it read. Ophie tried hard to hold back, but she could feel herself start to snuffle. She put the card facedown on the table.

"Don't you want to open it?"

Ophie shook her head, ignoring the tears streaming down her face.

"Oh, dear. I'm sorry. Wrong thing, huh?" Mrs. Peeler ran her hand down Ophie's hair. "You have always been my happy girl," her mother said. "But it's so hard for me to figure out what you're thinking lately. Especially because you don't seem to want to tell me . . ."

"I know," Ophie whispered.

"So, sweetie," said Mrs. Peeler, handing Ophie a pink napkin, "I just want to let you know that I love you dearly . . ." Her mother was tearing up too. "Even if I can't always understand you, I still always, always love you. Very much."

Ophie handed her mother the other pink napkin and fell into her arms. "Me too, Mom," she said, crying until her shoulders shook. It hurt and felt good at the same time, this thing inside her breaking open. "I love you so much too. And Daddy. And even Callie. So much."

Chapter Twelve

On the day of the field trip, Ophie still hadn't opened the letter from Lizzy. She knew that once she read it, she'd have to tell Lizzy that she was staying in Oregon forever. It would be official. Real. Then Lizzy, like the ruby shoes, would be something that didn't fit her anymore, just another souvenir for the memory closet. So Ophie just placed the letter in her desk and tried to pretend to look forward to today's field trip.

At school, she still had the TV Girls. Rachel and Merry sat by Ophie in the back of the bus.

But during the hour-long ride, all Rachel did was talk with Merry. Ophie got tired of craning her neck. "Uhhhhh. This trip is taking forever," said Merry.

"I'm dying of boredom," said Rachel.

Me too, thought Ophie.

Merry reached into her lunch sack and pulled out a special pink sandwich bag. It was full of Hershey's kisses. *XXX from Mother* was written in felt pen on the side. "Want one?" she said.

"Ooh! I have something to share too!" Ophie said, perking up. As the girls each took a chocolate, Ophie dug into her own lunch sack and pulled out a little brown paper bag. She reached in and pulled out a tiny, orange, egg-shaped fruit. "Kumquat?" she said.

"What is *that?*" asked Merry, frowning.

"Kumquats!" said Ophie. "I used to have a tree full of them in my old backyard!" She took the fruit, popped it into her mouth, and chewed.

"Eeeeeeeew!" said Merry. "Aren't you going to peel it?"

"You don't peel it," said Ophie.

"You EAT the SKIN?" said Rachel.

"Eeeeeeeeeeew!" said Merry and Rachel together.

Ophie stopped chewing. Finally, she choked down the fruit and said weakly, "Well, you eat grape skins and apple skins . . ."

"Totally sick," said Merry.

And according to Merry and Rachel, everything at the Pioneer Museum was "totally sick" too. Roasting a jackrabbit over a fire, wearing a dirty dress on the trail, going to the bathroom outdoors, eating cornmeal mush fried in fat—all of it sick, sick, sick.

Ophie looked at the diorama of the woman in the stained calico dress bent over a campfire, coyotes howling on a distant mountain, and thought, "Those girls must have been so brave!" She imagined the statue coming to life and yanking Merry Morshak by her perfect hair bow.

"When the first pioneers came here over the Oregon Trail, none of them knew what would come next!" said Miss Fast. "Some had had guides, and many set out in groups, but they still had to be ready for anything."

As Ophie listened to Miss Fast's description of the Oregon Trail, she couldn't help but think that it made walking down the yellow brick road look pretty easy. "A change in the weather, sick oxen, an accident or an illness in the family—these were extremely dangerous things," Miss Fast said. "You had to be tough to be a pioneer, and adaptable and a quick thinker."

Ophie tried to picture the TV Girls on the trail, arguing over who got to ride Thunder or Windy. At night they'd sit around a campfire and whine some while the coyotes closed in.

Lizzy, on the other hand, would be a perfect pioneer and campfire companion. They'd take turns with each other, one playing the harmonica while the other friend sang. As for Merry and Rachel? *I'd pull out my old harmonica, and they'd tell me to put "that stupid thing" back in my pocket.*

Then Ophie caught a glimpse of Brittany, bent over, inspecting a plow. *Look at that girl!* she thought. So, maybe Brittany wouldn't be able to handle a duet on the harmonica. But Ophie was sure that if a horse died, Brittany Borg would—well, *just pull the wagon by herself!*

Ophie watched the back of Brittany's head as the class filed in for "Pioneer Theater." She began to follow her, until Merry yanked her arm.

"We're sitting up here," said Merry, pointing to a high corner of the bleachers.

Ophie followed them into the rafters, dragging her feet.

When everyone was seated, the lights went out. And there, at center stage, appearing in a spotlight, was a man in a beat-up leather hat, a bandana, and dirty pants. His teeth were clamped down on a corncob pipe. His only furniture was a tree stump.

"Hello young'uns!" said the pioneer, taking the pipe from his mouth. "My name's Rastus. Welcome to the year 1860!"

"Rastus?" said Brittany.

"Yes, missy?" Rastus said.

"Smoking is bad for you."

Ophie sat up and leaned forward in her seat.

"Yes, ma'am," said Rastus. "But we don't know that yet—a-way back here in 1860." The pioneer put the pipe back between his teeth and grinned. "Now, as I was a-gonna say, things are different back here in 1860. The only fuel our wagons run on is oxen power and mule power and horse power—"

"A car runs on horsepower," volunteered Brittany.

Ophie felt a little smile cross her lips.

"I'm afeared," said the pioneer, "I don't know what you mean by CAR—*this being 1860.*"

"I saw you drive up in a Hyundai," Brittany said.

Ophie glanced over at the TV Girls and quickly put her hands over her mouth to hide her smile.

"Hmmm, *welll* . . . Back in 1860"—the pioneer raised his voice a notch and looked at Miss Fast—"children raised their hands when they wanted to ask a question. That gone outta style, or what?"

"Oh, brother," Merry muttered, shifting in her seat.

"It's like she stays up all night and thinks of dumb things to say." Rachel sighed.

"Why can't she just be quiet?" whined Merry.

Ophie dropped her hands from her mouth. "BECAUSE SHE DOESN'T WANT TO!" she said.

Merry jumped in her seat.

And Ophie thrust her hand in the air and waved as if she were a shipwrecked person flagging down a passing plane.

"Oh, put it down!" Merry said.

But instead Ophie looked right at Merry and stood up. "Rastus," she said, "are *you* in 1860 by yourself, and we're still in modern times? Or are we all in 1860 together?"

"Lemme see," Rastus said, scratching his beard. "I reckon I'm in 1860, and you all are in modern times. Okay?"

"Well, if I was a pioneer in 1860 and I walked into a room full of people from the twenty-first century, you know what? I'd want to find out about the future!"

"You would, wouldja? And what's so all-fired special about the future?"

"Did you know," Ophie said, "that nowadays, they can put a pig's heart in a human and women can vote?"

"Sit down!" hissed Rachel.

"Well I'll be dad-blasted," Rastus said. "Who'd-a thought it? Gals vote?" Dazed, he took a seat on the stump.

"We took pictures on Mars!" Tyler yelled.

"NO!" Rastus said.

"We cloned a sheep from another sheep!" said Laura.

"Yer pullin' muh leg!" said Rastus.

"Policemen can tell who you are just by looking at your spit!" shouted Robin, totally ignoring the TV Girls' *"Sssssssshhhh!"*

"I'll be flat, dead-dog flabbergasted!" said Rastus, scratching his head. "And GIRLS can

VOTE? Please! No more!" he warned. "The old ticker can't take it."

"Ophie Peeler, if you don't sit down right now . . ." Merry's eyes practically boiled.

"I'm sorry, Merry," Ophie said coolly. "I have just one more thing to tell Rastus."

"Oh all righty," said Rastus, breathing heavily. "But just ONE more." He clutched his chest.

"GIRLS CAN BE PRESIDENT!" Ophie roared.

Rastus got up, staggered, put two hands over his heart, and fell to the ground.

Screams and laughter erupted from the class—including one completely unbottled belly laugh . . . from Ophie!

"Quick!" said Ophie, running to the stage. "Brittany Borg, can you do CPR?"

"Yes, I can!" said Brittany.

"Well, come on!" Ophie said.

Ophie panicked a little when she spotted Miss Fast rushing toward the stage. But Rastus opened one eye, lifted his head, and shooed her

away. Rastus gave an OOF! as Brittany straddled his ribs.

"Out with the bad air! In with the good,"
chanted Ophie, checking her wristwatch.

"OUT WITH THE BAD AIR! IN WITH THE
GOOD!" chanted some of the other kids.

Brittany pressed down on the pioneer's
chest. Rastus shook. He threw up a leg. Finally
he spluttered. He was alive!

"Why, you two gals saved my life!" he said,
wiping his brow. He rose and shook both Ophie's
and Brittany's hands. He turned to the crowd
and lifted his fist. "GIRL POWER!" he said. He
led the girls to sit on the corner of the stage. "A
place of honor," he called it.

Ophie and Brittany stepped from the spotlight into the shadows. They sat down next to
each other cross-legged.

Rastus pretended to dust off his hands.
"Now, boys and girls, do you think we might
talk about 1860?"

Ophie tried to make out Brittany's face in
the dark. "I'm sorry," she whispered.

"Good," Brittany said.

"Oh, Brittany," said Ophie, "that's just like you!"

"Tana's mad, though," said Brittany.

"She should be," Ophie said.

"She told me every time she sees you, she wishes she could bite you."

"She should," said Ophie.

"But she won't," Brittany said.

Ophie knew that. Ophie also knew that Brittany would say yes when she asked to sit with her on the bus. And that Tana would forgive her. But that wasn't enough.

Ophie reached into her pocket. "Kumquat?" she said.

"Sure." Brittany popped the fruit into her mouth and chewed contentedly.

A warmth spread over Ophie. Already she had ideas for truly earning Brittany's friendship—*a different kind of friendship she was used to. But still,* she thought, *still really good.*

First, though, there's something else I gotta do.

Dear Lizzy:

You are not the only one who wants me to come back to Long Beach. I wanted to come back too. (We are so much alike!) Except now I have to tell you something. My dad has a job here in a office and we are going to be in Oregon a long time. For a while I was so mad. He was one city to late!!

You asked me what it's like here. It is quiet and serious and rainy. There isn't any one to sing with but these 2 girls who are snobby. But once you get used to it there are some nice people. Like this one friend I have named Brittany. I think you would like her, but maybe not right away.

Lizzy—I want you to have the ruby shoes, which you all ready know if you looked in the box. I tried them on and they don't fit anymore. Plus they arent really Oregon shoes. I think they more belong down there with you and your smaller feet, your singing, and all that bright sunshine. In Oz!

Please write back soon!!
Love, love, love,
Your friend forever,
OPHIE PEELER

xxx

I would like to gratefully acknowledge Cecile Goyette for her expertise, inspiration, and sense of humor. I also salute my comrade-in-writing, Russ Nelson, for his emergency problem-solving skills and unflagging optimism. Heartfelt thanks to you both.